A Cannibal and Melancholy Mourning

Catherine Mavrikakis

A Cannibal and Melancholy Mourning

translated by
Nathalie Stephens

Coach House Books

Originally published in 2000 as *Deuils cannibales et mélancoliques*
    by Editions TROIS , Montreal

first English edition

Published with the assistance of the Canada Council for the Arts and the Ontario Arts Council. The publisher also acknowledges the Government of Ontario through the Ontario Book Publishing Tax Credit Program and the Government of Canada through the Book Publishing Industry Development Program.

NATIONAL LIBRARY OF CANADA CATALOGUING IN PUBLICATION

Mavrikakis, Catherine, 1961-
[Deuils cannibales et mélancoliques. English]
    A cannibal and melancholy mourning / Catherine Mavrikakis ; translated by Nathalie Stephens.

Translation of: Deuils cannibales et mélancoliques.

ISBN 1-55245-140-2

    I. Stephens, Nathalie, 1970- II. Title. III. Title: Deuils cannibales et mélancoliques. English.

PS8576.A8579D4813 2004   C843´.6   C2004-901429-3

To a,

To e,

To i,

To o,

To u,

To y,

To you,

To Hervé.

No, the living have no pity on the dead
And what would the dead do with the pity of the living
For the heart of the living is hard as a living tree
    and they go their strong and vivid way
Though the heart of the dead lies bleeding
    and stricken with grief
And all a prey to blows, too open to blows
    with its uncovered carcass
For the living going their way have no pity on the dead
Who remain with their hearts uncovered to the wind

        'La mort grandissante'
        — Saint-Denys Garneau, tr. John Glassco

I learn of the death of my friends much as others discover their lottery ticket still doesn't have the winning number. This week I lost yet another Hervé and it was statistically predictable: all of my friends are named Hervé and are, for the most part, HIV-positive.

Death by statistics delivers us from nothing. Certainly not from the unpredictability of death.

I haven't gotten used to death. I never see it coming. Hervé's death goes splash! Just splash and it's over … A splash that keeps making me jump. One repetitious splash.

Survivor guilt, and yet I too will die. It's statistically predictable. But what kind of certainty does that grant?

When I mentioned Hervé's name to Flora, I knew to expect the worst. Her hand began immediately to seek out the corner of the table and her body bent dangerously under the weight of words she could barely speak: 'It's terrible, terrible for his parents.' I believe she was thinking of her own children, Hervé's age, her children who are now parents, her children, well inscribed into her lineage, whom she wants never ever to see die. And me, all I could think of were Flora's worries, her family, weddings, births and, far away, at the back of my mind, I could only just see Hervé, in very small. Hervé dead. Some vague thing. Hervé lying on a daybed. His body, ten years younger, already thin, in a dignified pose – that, I suppose, conferred by death and embalmers. 'It happened so quickly,' stammered Flora in tears. 'He hadn't said a thing to his parents, not a word. Nothing. And then, one week before his death, he had them sent for. It's funny, isn't it, that exclusion? And then at the last minute ... It just goes to show ... ' The image of Hervé becomes confused with that of another Hervé, dead two years ago, whom I had to see exposed to the four winds in his black coffin and his grey shirt. Hervé is dead. And it's the body of another Hervé that returns to haunt me, as Flora explains between sobs how her son Benjamin announced the death of Hervé. 'The death of Hervé.' How much longer will I have to keep hearing this? Yet it's a well-known scenario. A familiar word. Too familiar. Whose meaning I forget with each Hervé who dies. 'Hervé was at our daughter's wedding last summer, and yet he seemed well ... It just goes to show ... ' What was Hervé doing at a fucking wedding? He who hated families, happy unions, and could tolerate only my silence and my douleur de vivre. What was he doing at Marie's wedding, when he knew he was ill and would soon be dead, when he could speak of his illness to no one and under no circumstances? Whatever possessed him to set foot at the wedding of that twit, Marie, he who could only sabotage other people's conjugal bliss? What was he thinking? That I can never know because when it comes to death I know only what I have learned from my friends, dead or ill, and they've never told me how to understand the incoherence of our lives and of our deaths. With them, I learn to understand nothing, and most of all I learn not to understand their deaths. I refuse to understand. I refuse to abide by the law of some such knowledge, of a possible

12

reason. Death is scandalous. There's nothing I can do about it. That's the way it is.

When it comes to death, I'm a dunce, I'm a moron, I'm thick as a brick.

I must be giving Flora my crazy look, my hysterical look, my mad look, the look of someone in the throes of great anguish who has entered into a pact with the devil, because I can sense her growing fear of me. She asks me to sit down. While looking hard at her through my hollow eyes, which are still wandering the edges of my mind over something resembling Hervé's ridiculously minuscule, shrivelled body, I dare to ask, 'How did Hervé die?' I know the answer by heart for having heard it regarding so many Hervés. But with each Hervé, I want to hear it again. I have a possessive desire for that word which reassures and disgusts me with its cloying familiarity. I desire: AIDS. That's the word Flora mutters, or maybe I'm the one who pronounces the word that is enemy and life companion. Maybe I'm the one who speaks, or it's AIDS that speaks through me, through Flora and life at large. Because it seems to me that for years we say nothing other than AIDS – it devours, it ventriloquizes us.

The image of Hervé disappears, as though consumed by photographic acid. I see a grave, flowers petrified by frost. The hardness of stone. Crosses. Grey. Nothing. The cemetery. The name 'Hervé.' That's all. Hervé's surname is already gone from my memory and yet Flora hasn't stopped repeating it since the beginning of this absurd conversation.

'Where is Hervé buried?' The question moves through my body, and I squirm in my chair up, down and from left to right. Here I am, made into a witch at the stake of truth, a witch who cannot stop writhing, possessed as she is. And in front of the witch, Flora continues to speak, to hold forth, as though nothing were the matter, about Hervé's parents; she can't stop herself from giving news of a sadness, a very great sadness. 'Where is Hervé?' I say, panic-stricken by the meaning of such dismal and particularly derisory words. 'At the Montmartre cemetery.' Of course. There, of course, where Hervé always wanted me to accompany him on his walks, and where I so often refused to go. At the time, I found that strolling around the cemetery was too convergent with my dramatic doubts, with my mad desires for violent deaths, with my wild attempts at spectacular suicides. Strolls through the cemetery were dangerous for me. My own dreams were strewn with cadavers; I saw night and earth open and swallow me, so close to the stone tomb, I refused to play with death anymore, to let myself be seduced by its calm, its gravity. You're nothing but a fucking cocksucker, Hervé! From now on I have to go and visit you in Montmartre on my trips to France. Now I am forced to go the cemetery. And what's more, you won't even be there to laugh at my fears and superstitions, my insanity, you won't be there to call me to the futile order of death. I'll walk that road alone. Alone or perhaps with Olga, and maybe even the dog, if dogs are allowed in French cemeteries, which I doubt. They must go completely mad, with all those bones sealed into stone, and especially with that strong odour of rotting flesh, which likely makes them salivate and drool all the more.

Hervé hated dogs, if I remember correctly. Our tastes disappear so quickly after death. If Hervé did hate dogs, as in my memory, visiting his grave with my dog will be my revenge. I need to make Hervé pay for his death. I need to insult him. To spit on his grave, or to have my dog piss on his epitaph. I need, stupidly, to seek revenge. But for what?

It's been ages since Hervé 'neither should, nor could, nor would see me again.' It's been ages since he decided to drown me in the dark silence of his disappearance, to create in me, as he wrote last time, 'a malaise.'

At Hervé's first disappearance, I didn't react. I let time pass, the way one lets someone pass in front, out of courtesy. I held the intimate conviction that I would see Hervé again someday, that we would have it out. I didn't want to give in to Hervé's terrorism, to his frenetic desire to frighten me.

He enjoined me to speak to some truth, to speak à la Heidegger. He denied me gossip, distraction, futility, and I suspected that he wanted me to speak to him in German from time to time. I never liked Heidegger and I have no leanings whatsoever toward the Black Forest or, for that matter, roads that lead nowhere. I only like travel by airplane or by spaceship and dreary cities where people die face first against the concrete of murky sidewalks. All my academic friends are Heideggerians. As for me, I like talking, and, what's more, yelling, when I have nothing to say; I am allergic to German, it reminds me of war movies I watched as a child, and I despise Greek, poetry and the countryside.

Anyway, I couldn't ever be a Heideggerian, even if I wanted to. Heideggerians would denounce me pronto. The unveiling of being bores me to tears, and Hervé also bored me when he dove into his philosophical delirium. I preferred listening with him to Mahler and his

Kindertotenlieder. Together, we would criticize the inane and comatose air music lovers espouse, the same look that musicians acquire with devotional intensity.

When it came to music, we could have a laugh, since Hervé was an excellent musician. But he was also a very bad philosopher. I know how infuriated he would be to read these words; I know he would resent me for thinking that way, I know he'd call me a bitch, a cow, an illiterate and a dumb shit. That's where my betrayal lies, from the first lines of these talkative pages; it's in me. And, very strangely, I know that Hervé too is a traitor. But despite his betrayals, his silences and his disappearances, I know that he loved me. Just as I love him – I love him madly through my verboseness, just as I loved him through my unprofound and sullen silence which lasted several years.

Hervé's curse hit me with his first disappearance. I know he cursed me for not having answered his breakup letter. I know that he hated me for leaving him alone with his rage, but what did you want? For me to become a Heideggerian? I know you hated me for not being on your level, or, rather, for refusing the pure air of your German mountains, which give me vertigo. I know that you forgot me, wishing the worst on me, praying for my death. But I also know that when we crossed paths in Paris without exchanging a word, after several years of silence, in the movie theatre where they were showing Fassbinder's *The Bitter Tears of Petra von Kant*, you were there for me. You knew I was playing a major role in that film, a role you hoped never to see me play again. At *Petra* we could have become friends once more, but at our chance encounter, between you who never went out, and me who lived 5,000 km away from the Halles cinema (and from all of civilization, or so you thought), everything was said: 'One day, we will be able to acknowledge how much we loved one another in the absurd and tragic power of our shared hatred, in the cutting passion of our mutual rage.'

Hervé, your curse hit me right in the face. I had well over seven years of bad luck and you were likely right to curse me. I know that in death you continue to do so. I know you're capable of that. Of course you are. Every day delivers a different stroke of bad luck. You should be happy, you can contemplate with joy the spectacle of my misfortune. I know that you would be absolutely delighted at the face I made when Flora told me of your death. You loved seeing me speechless, haggard, disoriented, as close as possible to being. As for you, I'd rather hold on to your kindness, your love. And it's your love that I'm inscribing here. What you don't know is that my life is also written among the words you gave me, among the dreams in which you had me live. And when I did find happiness, it was you I wanted to write to. It was as you had predicted. You wouldn't like Olga, you would hate the dog, you would curse the cat. You would denounce my idiocy, my beliefs, my fevers, my fervour, my tenderness and my cruelty. I wanted to call and tell you everything, to add something to your long list of recriminations, accusations and truth especially, but I was waiting for the right moment. So, it seems you're dead. You told me you would be old one day. Maybe you were old, that old age conferred by illness that Hervé Guibert talked about shortly before his own death. Did you read Hervé Guibert? Did you know that for years I have been working on him? Of course, it was for you and you know it even if I didn't know anything about your AIDS. And, despite your death, here I am inventing the auspicious moment of our reunion. Time staged our separation, but I reject time, history, and I am conversing here, now, with you. The only conversations to be had are with the dead, with Mahler or with those who are now silent. I hope that while you were alive, I represented someone dead with whom you chatted from time to time, I hope that I answered you and that I made missed appointments with you in some Parisian movie theatre. Telepathy of the dead we were to one another.

Hervé, I'm taking on your curse. I'm turning it into cries, I'm turning it into tears that you never stopped shedding for me despite your imprecations and your violent silence. I'll make it into a spray of flowers and lay it on your grave.

'Would you like me to drive you home, Catherine? I'm leaving,' said Flora, suddenly digging her eyes into mine, as if to reach something in me resembling reason. 'No, that's very kind, I'll walk. What did Hervé do? What was his new job?' 'He was in advertising. You didn't know?' No, I didn't know that Heideggerians could one day move into advertising. Did Hervé laugh at his lost innocence? Did he think of me and my futility when he accepted such a job? I wouldn't be surprised.

With Flora gone, I find myself smack in the middle of a party at Bob's where all the guests unconsciously avoid approaching the wingback chair in which I reel, in which I capsize, in which I will end up drowned. I would like to get up and most of all to call Olga. Tell her of Hervé's death.

Talk to Olga who is at home with the animals and who will take me in her arms, she to whom all I do is bring home heaps of dead. Cartloads of them.

At Bob's, they all speak English and suddenly I can't remember the word for 'telephone.' I try in French. They seem to understand me. Another death to announce, another death to inter. I have become the cemetery of our deceased friends. Watch out, you better stop croaking, I'm almost full to capacity.

Olga's voice wraps around me, understands me, awaits me; Olga's voice will clean me of my tears. Here I am now, holding Bob, that giant, in my arms. I am smothering him under the weight of all my dead Hervés, and I'm yelling into his ear, gripping his jacket clumsily: 'You take care of yourself.' Bob watched all of his friends die, so he knows that when I hold people like this to the point of strangulation, it's because Hervé is dead. I look for my bag, I don't find it. I make up my mind anyway and set out again suddenly, hysterically, on the highway of grief where I'm doing 160 kilometres an hour, where I'm driving furiously, my hair in the wind, my heart heavy with the death of other people. I take off like a shot, one friend lighter, one death heavier. 'I am a graveyard that the moon abhors.'

On the street, I want to sing my head off, I want to squeal my tires, to cry, to howl your name: Hervé! You often told me I could carry a tune, but how useless was that ability since in your view I had no voice. And it's true, I don't have the voice I need to shatter the world beneath cries of your name.

It's still sunny and this mild June violently rocks the road as it flashes by at full speed. June: the month of the dead.

But I could just as easily say that of July, August, December, April and the whole calendar. And why not insitute entire years as years of the dead? Every day I drive over the barely cold bodies of my deceased friends. And me, I run down everything in my path. I lean on the pedal of life. Full tilt.

Five years ago, on the trip from Québec to Baie-Saint-Paul, the taxi driver, a totally hyper guy, confided to Olga and me that the road on which we were happily doing close to 200 an hour was nicknamed, and with good reason, the highway of death. This guy had already buried nineteen of his friends, twelve of whom died on this road. For a thirty-year-old, having seen so much death over the course of one's existence was quite an accomplishment, and I wondered whether he wasn't better suited than me to write a book about the dead. I've resigned myself, I have no claim over it. There will always be someone more competent or more talented than me in this department. Death is unfortunately not an exclusive domain.

While the driver led us, at death-defying speeds, along a pilgrimage through all the intersections at which his friends had left their lives, I noted death's association with arithmetic, I thought of how much death is now managed mathematically. Insurance companies know all about that. Of all the countries in the world, Canada is where people have the most insurance. For everything: theft, fire, life, death, illness, poverty. Everything. Québec has among the highest rates of suicide and deodorant consumption per capita. Does that indicate some particular thing, draw a particular conclusion, instigate some particular mode of reasoning? Statistics — they are said to speak for themselves and I believe it. Mathematics and death — these two entities maintain a close relationship and I don't believe, like Heidegger, that bureaucracy, or for that matter accounting, veils our relationship to being when it comes to death. On the contrary — statistics are one part of a tragic destiny. In my opinion, they embody the remains of a kind of predestination which has become collective.

A young twenty-year-old woman is killed just outside my window by a seventy-nine-year-old driver. She had just finished her studies, found work as an actuary for an insurance company. In fact, she had just been put in charge of accidental deaths. Thus she was working on the statistics of her own death. Numbers don't mean anything?

The cab driver tells Olga and me how lucky he is to have survived an accident in which his brother died in his place. But he seldom speaks of his brother's death; he is happy to talk to us about his survival, to be here to impart his bullshit stories. The stupidity of survivors. The stupidity of my declarations throughout this book. To survive, as if that's all that mattered. The cabbie laughs because he is alive and, whereas Olga is not doing at all well, since she can't avoid thinking of her grandparents who live on the edge of this road of death which they have to take every day, I am thinking of Anne Frank. Who didn't survive, who didn't come back from the dead. Many people in the camps weren't gassed, but died of exhaustion, hunger, illness, fatigue, sadness, horror … Dead from not having been able to survive that. We musn't forget: death isn't all theatrical, death isn't all for Spielberg movies, death isn't all for classical music remixes. Most of all, there is death for nothing. In the movie *Anne Frank*

Remembered, Anne's childhood friend suggests that she might have survived had she known her father was still living. But since she believed her whole family was dead, she didn't struggle. Survive whom? What? For whom? For what? And for how long?

I will never know why Anne Frank was unable to survive, but I know that all the admirers of the late doyenne des Français, the oldest woman in France, petrify me with horror. There's something terrifying about the cult of survivors in the game of death. 'How wonderful that the doyenne des Français survived it all: the death of her parents, her friends, her brothers, her sisters, her children, her grandchildren and her great-grandchildren! Isn't it wonderful to have buried all those people and still want to carry on! How we would have liked to help her bury one or two more generations! Such hope for humanity. ' And all the while, my Hervés die in the most absolute silence, the silence of friends who are already dead.

Five years ago today, Hervé died, shredded in a London subway bombing. There was nothing left of his body, nothing at all, since the bomb was placed precisely under the seat on which he sat. At any rate, that's the official story. Hervé was most likely on the subway at 5:45 p.m. that October 31, 1991. Here, to celebrate Hallowe'en, we dress up like the dead. But in London, Hervé, who had lived for years in North America, was most likely taking the subway home after having spent the day at the British Library.

Hervé's mind was most certainly full of many thoughts not the least of which was his project to visit me the following week, because I have always found November to be a terrible month, the month of every death, and because Hervé wanted, in his usual fashion, to cheer me up. 'Take care!' he repeated over the telephone the last time he checked up on me. Hervé most likely died in tiny pieces scattered in the London Underground. Bombed by the terrorist group on which Hervé had written his thesis and which subsequently published an embarrassed press release. An irony of fate or the logic of destiny?

No grave on which to meditate, no cemetery to haunt on the Day of the Dead, no flower to buy. His memory flowers in me. I, who have very probably become the crypt of this dead friend.

I am a date machine, I am a mechanism of numbers and figures, I am the punching machine of days. I am among the most perfected of German devices – better yet, I am a computer that sounds at the beck and call of the past. Not a day goes by that isn't the commemoration of another. I know the birth and death dates of an incalculable number of people. And if by chance a day carries no reminder whatsoever, it's because it's the perfect day for a new catastrophe. Daytimes as well are haunted, full of ghosts, werewolves. They are heavy with the past. There is no way around it.

But my memory device is even more complex: I also remember the most futile and ancient of phone numbers. This aspect of my neurotic machinery is quite incomprehensible to me, although it constitutes yet another way for the past to inhabit me: very often, the number of a friend driven from my memory years ago resurfaces.

Hervé was born June 16, 1949; he died June 18, 1989. So he had just celebrated his fortieth birthday in hospital, and I imagine his room flooded with light, with abundant vegetation, giant flowers, lecherous, pornographic flowers offered to him. Once Hervé had dreamt of dying in the early morning, assassinated by a casual lover in a tourist room. I can see him dead on the morning of the 18th after a heated night with a man who slid into his bed and suffocated him in his embrace. Suffocation. That's how Hervé died. There's no doubt, there's even a Latin word for it, 'Pneumocystis carinii,' a talisman word, a fetish word that Hervé wrote to me, not without the pride that comes with naming a new lover. So 'Pneumocystis carinii' killed Hervé in the early morning, in the room full of flowers, flooded by the sun.

He wrote me June 14th, two days before his fortieth birthday, four days before his death: 'I don't think I admitted to you that I have AIDS. Yes, AIDS. And it attacks the lungs: Pneumocystis carinii.' It's true, I don't think Hervé had admitted his illness to me, even if his voice on the telephone June 12th sang a familiar song, the song of someone who can no longer breathe, the song of the beautiful swan Hervé seemed to incarnate. I don't think either of us had pronounced the word 'AIDS' a single time during our exchanges, and I find it especially hard to believe that Hervé didn't remember our mutual silence. But how does one admit to something? Because, like it or not, homosexuality is always a matter of admitting. Tell. Don't tell. Understand. Suggest. Do you hear me? Don't say anything. Know without words. Community of dead ones, of AIDS victims and gays. Community of admission, to do and redo. One would have to wear a badge all the time. And that wouldn't be enough, it would still be necessary to explain why, how, with whom, the first trauma and the last lover.

When Hervé first contacted me, after a laudatory review I had done of one of his plays, the editors of the paper for which I was working at the time thought it best not to slip Hervé's letter of thanks into my pigeonhole. After all, Hervé was so well known he had no need to thank such a mediocre creature as myself, a nuisance to my species. What's more, several months earlier, Hervé had insulted the entire editorial staff of the paper for not having found time to write a text they had promised to write. In the letter addressed to me and misplaced by the editorial staff, Hervé insulted the latter, sang my praises and ended up nearly deifying me for daring to 'stand up to that incompetent lot who stagnate in our institutions.' So I received Hervé's letter some four months after its dispatch date, with an explanatory note from my boss, Jean-François, apologizing for having inadvertently opened my mail and for having kept it on his desk all this time without realizing it. Jean-François added delicately that this series of events was of no importance since the sender did not request anything in particular.

When I received Jean-François's note and Hervé's letter, I quickly understood that Hervé was sick and that the newspaper office hoped he would die as soon as possible, in order to show that Hervé's views against a big American paper resulted from his illness and resentment. But since Hervé didn't die fast enough, and, as I later learned, left messages for me that I didn't return because they didn't reach me, Jean-François finally decided to give me Hervé's letter from which he had been unable to separate himself, and went to great lengths to make me understand that it was useless for me to answer my mail. Why did Jean-François let my article on Hervé go through? I don't know. Maybe he thought it a way of making amends with one of the best-known directors of our time? Was he simply being perverse? Maybe he wanted to see where all this fuss would lead. I don't know. But Hervé wasn't the sort to have a short memory.

Despite Jean-François, or thanks to him, I responded with great pleasure to Hervé's letter in which he announced to me, someone who didn't know him, that he was abandoning directing to devote himself to writing. Exhaustion, lack of time to complete projects, the ephemeral quality of directing, all led him to leave the stage. On receiving this news, I knew right away that Hervé was talking to me of his legacy and that I would play the role of executor. Why did I understand this right away? Why did he designate me? Because of words, of adjectives that I had chosen to speak in the paper of what was to be his last production, because of words and silences especially that pulsed in my review. Because of my tone, because of my name, I don't know.

And this is how Hervé first admitted his illness to me. So I answered Hervé, weighing each one of my words, so that he would know that I knew, but that I would speak of this knowledge only once he ended the game of innuendo. I made sure to leave him my telephone number and awaited his call for several days.

On the phone Hervé burned with his passion to tell. Each sentence tried to describe everything to me, in each word vibrated his whole past life and all his hope for a future life. We spoke for hours, and I was only too happy to find in this world a more fragile and nervously anguished person than me. I recognized that gasp in his voice when Hervé called me June 12, 1989, six days before his death, four days before his birthday, two days before writing me that letter in which he spoke to me begrudgingly, I'm sure of it, of 'Pneumocystis carinii'; but it had become unbearable to hear that gasp, hiccuping, whistling. Hervé was almost unable to breathe, but in each of his weak exhalations, I could still hear his feverish life, unable, as it was, to expel itself. Very simply, Hervé died consumed by his own energy, which his illness no longer allowed him to expend: 'Pneumocystis carinii' is its name.

Someone put up a 'For Sale' sign in front of my building. I've been wondering for several days who has decided to leave. A dream I had last week offers an answer. It's my old neighbour downstairs who is leaving. She handed her space over to someone with AIDS whose face is covered in Kaposi. He takes me on an extended tour of the apartment I had until now only glanced at furtively. I note how mouldy the apartment smells, but I pretend to like it for this new friend who asks if I will be there when he'll really need me. Dazed, I say yes. I go back home, just upstairs, and I have the terrible sense that I am walking on a grave. Not a French grave but one of my own, one that is covered in grass or snow. Those lawn-graves whose sponginess yields underfoot after a rainstorm. I am walking on my neighbour's grave. It's awful. I hope it doesn't open up and engulf me. I awake terror-stricken.

Most incredible of all is that during the week following my dream, I learn that it's my upstairs neighbour, whom I don't know, who is truly living with AIDS. But since one strange event leads to another, Fabrice, somewhat of a friend and HIV-positive, who walked past my place and saw the 'For Sale' sign, asks me to find out about the free apartment. 'I'd really like to live underneath you,' he tells me. How does he know that I dreamt him underneath me in that cursed apartment? In reality, I still don't even know which of the three apartments is coming free. I am quick to dissuade Fabrice. I have a vague sense that I should be the one moving out. But I can only stay: that much I know.

Dreams straddle one another, repeat themselves to become better entangled: last night, Olga and I were in a big room in a Parisian airport. On the ground, perched atop one another, dozens of sick men. With AIDS. Of course. All very weak, dressed in black. Faded black. With Olga, I must prepare them for the flight. I bring them home with me, to take better care of them. They are so slow, their gestures so fragile, so tenuous, that we are going to miss the airplane, the only one that will take us to the house. Must I leave them all there, all my sick friends, and think of myself, my return? Must I abandon them so that they can take flight toward their own skies, as one of them seems to suggest? I decide all of a sudden to not bring them with me, to strand them there—I won't follow the path they've opened to me. I won't travel with them. Not yet. I wake up in tears.

Despite my desire to pitch everything, I don't completely abandon my friends with AIDS. I resume writing about Hervé. It is what it is. But it frees me from nothing. On the contrary, I become more and more melancholy, possessively jealous of my dead.

When we met in a café on the east side of the city, I didn't know what to expect physically. Even though Hervé had been on every television, here and elsewhere, by some strange fate I never saw him. But I was incapable of admitting that to Hervé on the telephone and I answered yes when he said, 'Anyway, you'll recognize me. I'll see you in an hour at the café.' Right away, I called my friend Isabelle who had taken acting lessons from him and had her describe him to me. She was only able to provide the colour of his eyes and hair and his height, so that I found myself smiling nervously and stupidly at every tall man with somewhat brown hair who walked through the door.

Hervé had arranged to meet me at a guys' café – in other words, a café for gay men – and when I felt his hand on my shoulder, I understood that Hervé wasn't a seer but that I was simply the only girl in the café, something I hadn't yet realized, preoccupied as I was with craning my neck to catch sight of all the tall dark-haired men who were taller than the others by a head. Hervé was indeed tall, he had brown eyes and brown hair, but what struck me was the stiffness of his black leather clothes. Hervé was a tough guy, something his hurried voice never suggested to me. There was, nonetheless, something imprecise, overflowing, about Hervé's hand on my shoulder. Hervé was too, too full of himself and he contaminated me with his excess. The café was soon filled

31

with Hervé's presence, with his words, his gaze. He burst open the space, the walls; the whole world seemed too cramped for him and here he was, tacitly demanding that I help him to contain a bit of that madness of being, just a little, so that he could write a book and bear to die.

In me, Hervé had found his double – the same spasms, the same fitful splintering of his person that he could hardly contain in the rigidity of his black leather – and he asked this double to hold his hand in order to find in himself a tangible place from which it would be possible to leave. 'For me, dying has always meant exploding on board a spaceship launched full-tilt against the emptiness of space, and I don't want that anymore, do you know what I mean?' Yes, finding the right metaphor for his death, that's what Hervé asked of me in that gay café, one Tuesday afternoon when we saw one another for the first and last time. He hoped I would help him write the appropriate metaphor of death, one that would tell the truth, that would appease the wounds inflicted on our flesh by the speed of living. The metaphor that theatre could not give him and that only writing promised. Writing ... and me. Me: his road to death. Me: executor of his posthumous books. Me: his literary critic. Me: memory of writing and speech. Me: Catherine, who would always have the courage to tell him the value of his work, who would make him live on after his death. Me: Catherine. Me: literature.

I was utterly disarmed by the magnitude of Hervé's request. I didn't know how to help him appropriate his death nor how to make him speak words of passage toward infinity or emptiness. What had struck me about his productions was precisely what they could teach me about the theatricality of the dead body, about the derisory artifice and pomp of our cadavers. Hervé's plays made people laugh incessantly, but a paralyzing laugh, a laugh that could at any moment freeze us, overcome us with horror. The horror of our own end.

That Hervé delivered his imminent death to me in veiled terms and spoke of my capacity to help him 'move through to the other side of the mirror' (since that's the metaphor he used while scrutinizing me with his big brown doubtful eyes, watching, searching for my approval) caught me completely off guard. The way he searched out my eyes, believed in me, forced me to resist him. It was like I moved into a space beside myself, like I was dislocated, and it was difficult afterwards to reconstruct the marks of the illness on Hervé's face, since all that came back to me that afternoon was Hervé's eyes in mine. His big eyes looking into me for signs of his death. Not the death that was visible in his sunken eye sockets, nor that which made the skin of his face stick to his bones, but the death that I would have him accomplish through writing and my literary severity, the death buried in me, the death I did not yet know myself capable of.

For over a year, Hervé called me once a week for a detailed resumé of my reading of his great book of death. What's more, he put me in charge of collecting texts that were already old and helping him rework them. These scattered texts were published six months after his death, as promised. Apparently, in his hospital room, he continued to edit his work, faithfully following my suggestions. But the great book of death remained incomplete; Hervé was unable to finish it. 'I hope at least to spend one last beautiful summer writing on the patio of my new apartment. We'll see. I don't know if, like Proust, there will be time enough,' Hervé wrote to me from the Hôtel-Dieu Hospital, June 14, 1989. The metaphor Hervé had dreamed of for his death could not take form: I was unable to be there to help him find the moment of his death. He called me June 12 with his breathless voice, told me he would be in the hospital for a few days for some insignificant thing and that he wanted me to be ready to dive back in as soon as he got out. June 14 he wrote me and revealed all about 'Pneumocystis carinii,' but I only received his letter on the 19th (I had moved June 1 without having had time to tell him and was having my mail forwarded). June 19, the day after his death. A letter from beyond the grave, a letter that I carry with me wherever I go, because the dead continue to talk to me and send me thoughts perfumed with eau du ciel, thoughts redolent with the smell of hell's burning stakes.

In this letter, Hervé entreats me to go see him in hospital, he who had refused to see me again after our first encounter, so that I wouldn't keep too frightening an image of him. So he invited me, in his letter, to go see him 'on the other side of the mirror,' and it's with his permission that I represent him here in death.

Nonetheless, I didn't see him in the hospital but in the funeral home, where Hervé, his lifelong lover, allowed me to accompany him. In fact, Hervé, Hervé's great love, is the one who announced Hervé's death to me, June 18 at 11 a.m. Since the 12th, the day of Hervé's phone call, I had spent horrible days, full of dreams of his death. June 17, after days spent hesitating, I wrote him a letter telling him that I couldn't stand his silence or mine anymore, that I had to go see him in hospital or at home and that we had to see one another again. June 18, I called Hervé, with whom I had spoken several times on the phone. I asked Hervé straight out if Hervé was there or still in hospital because I had a letter for him. I was very angry at Hervé and my words were quick, disconnected. Hervé, who in the end had become accustomed to the overflowing language his lover used, answered, 'Catherine, Hervé died early in the morning, six hours ago. I am here to make phone calls, funeral arrangements. Can you hold? There's someone on the other line.'

I waited on the phone for a very long time, devastated by the suddenness of Hervé's death, a death we had nonetheless never stopped preparing for together through that long year during which we met. Had Hervé also been surprised by his death? Did it startle him? Back on the phone, Hervé heard my sobs and apologized for his lack of savoir faire: 'I should have prepared you, I was loathsome.'

Hervé was so busy with funeral rituals that he managed to forget his own pain. He read me the list of things he had to do, the calls he had to make to everyone, and his obligation to attend Hervé's cremation, scheduled that very day at five p.m. Hervé had asked to be incinerated as quickly as possible, without people or speeches, but the funeral home required the presence of someone to witness the smooth progress of the cremation. 'A real ceremony will take place in several days, Hervé prepared everything, will you come?' That's when, I don't know how or why, I begged Hervé, whom I didn't know, to let me accompany him to the incineration of his lover's body. I had not yet received Hervé's letter in which he invited me to the hospital. Nonetheless, I received Hervé's message loud and clear and needed to see him, even dead. At the time, I had never yet seen any dead, except on TV, where the dead, both true and false, made me close my eyes. How did I find the courage and audacity to ask Hervé to see Hervé dead? I don't know, but Hervé, who knew Hervé much better than I, reassured me with his gentle voice and simply answered, 'Okay.'

We agreed to meet in front of the funeral home, where Hervé had to sign thousands of forms. On the walls, pictures of cemeteries, columbariums and several other funeral homes were meant to reassure us of the meaning of death. 'This is where it ends and, as you can see, it does end,' is what the photographs of these derisory monuments seemed to say, buildings built against death, right up against death, in an attempt to suffocate it. Tonnes of stone erected less to keep memory than to forget, to reassure. But is it really possible to be done with those we have known? Is there an end for our dead? I awaited from Hervé's body an answer to these questions. I still believed in death as an epiphany, as the potential revelation of some truth.

I thought that Hervé's dead body would deliver me from uncertainty and bring me some rest. But the soul's peace is not manifest in the bodies of those with AIDS nor in those of the dead. I have not yet seen dead old people, for whom death is a supposed deliverance inscribed in the peaceful pose the elderly assume in their coffins. All I have seen of my dead is the torment, the pain, the decomposition already present in the body stricken by illness or accident. I am waiting for the dead who will convince me of the gentleness of death. But for now, all I know is the silent movement of tortured bodies, the movement of unsculptured stone. I know the petrified chaos of the dead body, when I had been promised serenity and silence.

I touched upon the mystification of our discourses on death when I saw Hervé dead, dead and prepared for incineration. He was there in his coffin, sick more than ever, struggling more than ever, but caught in the impossible silenced gesture he would have wanted to set down against death. I saw Hervé furled by death's ruse, Hervé restricted. Everything in him was still governed by anger, but anger as impossibility. And this impossibility is unbearable; to me it constitutes the sense of madness I have before my dead. A desire to laugh or to howl because death is not of the realm of truth, of what's possible. It is only plausible and that's why it is so theatrical. Like in Hervé's plays.

Hervé's dead body is theatrical, the posture is full of affect and the movement that should arise from it doesn't occur. It is false, but plausible. Hervé is grey and Hervé is trying to make a joke; he is trying to make Hervé laugh but doesn't succeed and he in turn becomes petrified and petrifies his life. Hervé will not live long after Hervé's death; AIDS will declare itself to him violently. Hervé will die quickly, without Hervé to see him dead. Hervé will die alone and will want no one at his side. And you needn't be clairvoyant to know. You need only see Hervé attempt to lean toward Hervé's dead body and see his paralysis to know that the movement of life has stopped in him as well. The undertaker is in a hurry. He closes the coffin and the coffin leaves, carried slowly away by a mechanism worthy of the most beautiful plays produced by Hervé. The coffin slips away. Hervé and I remain, embarrassed by our uselessness. A small curtain closes. Death's modesty. Curtain. Curtain, I want to applaud. Hervé would have liked that. And if he had staged his incineration rather than write it down, it wouldn't have been more accomplished.

Suicide haunts me. I am Cary Grant in *North by Northwest*; I run fast and well, with elegance, and for now I am winning. I am the most agile. I have escaped my own death thanks to I don't know what miracle. One day my psychoanalyst said to me, laconically, 'You have never attempted suicide because you know you wouldn't botch the job.' It's true, I will not or would not botch my suicide. My life is alternately inscribed between the tenses: future, conditional. In the present: 'I do not commit suicide.' That I know. And I tolerate life, because I know that if necessary I will not or would not botch my suicide.

Suicidal thoughts are hereditary, passed along from father to daughter. I think they are transmitted through families much like the hemophiliac gene. Secret laws govern suicidal thoughts, I'm sure of it.

I have a totally hysterical friend who yells at me and shrieks that I am a coward the minute I start talking suicide. She believes that my ideas on the subject betray a weak mind. And yet today, in writing about suicide, I feel this to be an act of courage. Here I botch nothing. I am displacing temporality.

In the high-rise in which I used to live, a man threw himself from the window. Splash! A muted splash. A muffled splash. He was a psychoanalyst, adored Deleuze and committed suicide one month before his mentor, in the same way. A splash in the void. Knowledge or fore-knowledge of Deleuze's end? This psychoanalyst was also a pedophile. I knew it the first time I met him in the elevator. I'm not on a witch hunt, it's a matter of empathy, recognition. Something that's very common in some places, like building elevators. I must admit that I am also claustrophobic. He knew I had caught on to him and avoided me outright. A young neighbour we had in common tried to introduce us to one another. In vain.

The psychoanalyst committed suicide early in the morning by throwing himself from the window he always kept open in case the irrepressible desire to kill himself took hold. Like the urge to take a piss.

That morning my dog insisted on going out onto the balcony; she seemed feral, possessed, absolutely voracious without my knowing why. There, nine storeys below, was my neighbour's body, shredded by the railings on which he had impaled himself. My rabid dog, rendered desperate by the smell of blood, wanted to sniff the body and perhaps devour it, but I couldn't understand why all the fuss. I took Sud out immediately and determined that down below, police officers and firefighters had the building under siege. I had simply thought that Sud needed urgently to do her business, and it was only upon my return from our walk that I asked a building employee what was going on. 'A suicide,' he offered. I went back up to my apartment completely haggard and looked into the garden to see, to see something, see what had happened. I wanted to grasp what this looked like. In truth I didn't really know what I wanted to see. I expected to see traces especially, a theoretical reconstruction of the physical facts and causes of an abstraction: death. I had forgotten about the body, convinced as I was of the erasure of its presence by the representatives of the order of the living. Down below, firefighters chuckled and busied themselves around the pool. On one of the railings, an orange sheet floated vaguely. A piece of body sought, by the force of the wind, to escape from underneath the fabric. At that very moment I understood that the body was there and that Sud's panic-stricken rage had been provoked by the smell of the cadaver. After a quarter of an hour, during which I couldn't remove my eyes from the orange cloth and during which my dog seemed positively deranged, howling and shaking about diabolically on the balcony as if prepared to jump the nine storeys in order to reach her prey, I saw the firefighters move toward and lift the sheet. I was very high up and could see almost nothing of the body's details, but I couldn't stand to watch the unhooking of the cadaver from the railing. I understood that they would have to cut the body in two in order to remove it from the spikes. I resumed watching once the body had been reconstituted on its stretcher and when all that was visible was its head, small, grey-haired. The cadaver was carried away. My dog calmed down at last, and I spent days reviewing, in a decidedly obsessive and morbid way, all the inhabitants of the building in order to determine who had committed suicide. In the elevator, whenever I saw a neighbour whom I had previously thought dead, I would start talking to her or him with mad enthusiasm and hold open the elevator door, emphasizing the need to take care, as long as one was still alive. Hysterically, I carried the good word of health. My whole neighbourhood had become ghostly.

The porter relieved me of my anguish when he spoke to me of the incident of his own accord. I would never have dared to ask anything of anyone for fear of coming across as perverse, when obviously this story was driving me nuts.

The porter gave me a name, the name of the dead man, but I didn't know right away who it was. My young neighbour, the friend the psychoanalyst and I had in common, only ever spoke of the former by his first name, Hervé. It was only in the elevator, in fact, that the name of the dead person and the person of the psychoanalyst assumed the same shape, that of the cadaver I had barely seen the morning of the suicide. Everything fell back into place. Words and forms became tombstones. The ghost of the impaled dead vanished and my neighbours resumed their place in the world of the living. In fact, the death of the psychoanalyst, which until then I had interpreted as an act of despair or courage, appeared almost insignificant to me. I never liked that guy, and he gave as good as he got, but the obscenity of the cadaver death had offered me no longer seemed incongruous. I thought only of naming the dead and was relieved to have known the cadaver when it was still alive, for the body of a stranger would have disturbed me more. There was something reassuring about not having only seen the body dead. Something human that allowed me to think of that body in movement, and not just tossed about by the wind sweeping under the orange sheet that morning.

Only three months later did I understood the meaning this death held for me. A friend, also a psychoanalyst, to whom I had confided the death of our neighbour, told us that when she spoke of the suicide to a colleague, the latter immediately burst into tears. She then admitted to our friend that for twenty-two years she had carried a terrible secret, entrusted to her by my neighbour when he was a student, and that at long last she could speak.

My neighbour had been arrested for pedophilia in his youth and had received treatment ever since. My friend's colleague was convinced he had killed himself in remorse or abjection. But on the same day on which these words were reported to me, I learned in confidence from my neighbour that the psychoanalyst had committed suicide because a young man had rejected his advances, and his death had been motivated simply by passion and was far from being regret-filled. For all those who had known him, therefore, the official version of his death was the regret and shame that, in their minds, all pedophiles must have. This version of the facts was judged by all, and especially the neighbours in the building, to be moral, and they went so far as to take on a knowing look to evoke it. I noticed that my neighbour had spoken of his 'illness' to everyone and that people imagined him dead in peace, having found rest in his soul through atonement by death.

If he had detested me it wasn't because I knew, but because he hadn't been the one to tell me. He had not had the chance to confess his repentance to me, so typical in our psychologizing society where it is promised that talk frees us of the chains that constitute our problems, when in reality our admissions are driven by perversion and pure manipulation. 'Our repentance is base, And our confessions fatly earn their pay,' wrote Baudelaire. It takes one to know one.

My neighbour killed himself in the petty torments of an uncontrollable passion in order to hurt someone and not so as to free the earth of the 'bastard' he enjoyed embodying under the sad gaze of the universe. The expiatory version suited everyone except me. 'The poor man,' people murmured in a complicit tone. And me, I could only think of the rage that had motivated that act, rage at not being able to possess enough. Rage, and emotional blackmail especially, were patent in the suicide note he left to the man he wanted as lover and captive. This suicide held meaning for me. It taught me that I needn't lend noble causes to such an act, that we are often beside the truth when it comes to suicide and that whatever peace death brings to the soul is often an elaborate comedy played by the suicide. And perhaps not the last.

I learned to not always have compassion for suicides. Compassion I felt more or less obligated to have in the face of the suicide, several years ago, of my grandfather. The old man did himself in to piss us off, so that we couldn't cash in on his life insurance (which he had always promised my mother), and if he ended up dead, it was in fact a pure accident. Once again he thought himself able to make his body into the theatre of his supposed unhappiness. My grandfather had made several suicide attempts, each more dramatic than the last, and in the end, he botched the staging of his act, miscalculated his dosage of pills, and knocked himself off. No life insurance and a will that left everything to others.

The suicided neighbour allowed me to free myself completely from the death of my grandfather, and later, when one of my doctoral students, a depressive Bergman-esque Swede, threatened to commit suicide, I replied coldly, 'Fine, but not in my office,' to which I had lent him the key.

To me, suicide is neither cowardly nor courageous. It often much resembles life, and in the case of my grandfather, his suicide was just another failure and a scam.

What links must I draw between my AIDS dead and my suicides? And why do the first receive my utter affection and the second my utter indifference? I don't know.

And yet, I could just as easily end up AIDS-dead as I could suicided. At any rate, that's what I believe. That's how I accept my life, my love and my hatred of others.

One of my Hervés, upon learning of the evolution of his illness, shot himself in the head. And Hervé Guibert himself preferred to end things before the end, which was arriving in small underhanded and dreadful steps. If only my grandfather could have died of AIDS, how long I would have mourned him. Unfortunately for him, after the death of his wife, he slept exclusively with all of my cousins and sisters, his granddaughters, too young not to be sexual and narcotic virgins. At any rate, that's what my sister, completely terrorized by the potential ghost of my grandfather, confided to me at the time of my neighbour's suicide. The synchronistic coincidence of Hélène's confession and my neighbour's defenestration marked for me the beginning of a profound reflection on what is so abject about certain suicides and more generally what is so abject about the beyond. If, from his grave, my shyster of a grandfather continues to instill fear in my sister who has remained, by his fault, a little girl, I can only hope that he is terrorized by my contempt and my vengeance. From time to time, I go and spit on his grave, because I don't think he's keen enough, even dead, to read my thoughts. But he does understand blasphemy and abuse, he, that respectable, upstanding man, widowed so young and intent never to remarry so as not to tarnish the memory of my grandmother. I am the only one of his granddaughters to have been spared the grandfatherly libido. It's almost insulting. I carry the first name of my grandmother, his wife. It was perhaps a mark of respect for her, for him not to have touched me.

Let it be known to the bastard: neither ghosts nor incest frighten me.

My friend Hervé, who had just lost someone close, was home alone one night when he felt, all of a sudden, the very distinct presence of the dead he had buried several days prior. Hervé entreated him to go away. He explained that he wasn't ready for an apparition, that at that precise moment his mental health couldn't withstand such a shock and that this manifestation of the beyond impeded his ability to mourn appropriately. He presented his case so brilliantly that the ghost, convinced, left docilely to go and haunt a more psychologically prepared individual. Because of this event, Hervé remained convinced, for a very long time, of his power over the dead, which turned him into somewhat of a megalomaniac. For a long time he believed that he was in control of death, until he was carried away by AIDS at the age of twenty-five.

For some of the living, into which category I fall, the dividing line between the world of the living and that of the dead sometimes seems so vague that I see myself as a living-dead. It's not just that I am obsessed with death. It's more that I start to think like the dead, to understand the anger some of them hold. To see the world from their point of view. And although it may seem that this leads me to achieve a sort of detachment from life and earthly goods, instead I have the impression of embodying myself, of sinking into the opacity of things. Without the dead I would be ethereal.

But since in order for the dead to speak to us, they must often make do with the language and the world of the living, I keep an eye out for their presence in the hardness, in the asperity of all things. That is perhaps what is referred to as the memory of objects, history or being. It's my becoming-dead that attaches me to living.

In the elevator of my building, every now and then, I encounter time and its madness, time and its sovereign madness. Each time the door opens, I meet a neighbour I haven't seen for a day or six months. The tyranny of arbitrary encounters keeps me hanging. With the elevator, I measure the dementia of time without being able to establish a true temporal logic. What is vague, delirious, remains in the form of questions and near-certainties: 'Here is the couple I haven't seen for so long, how they've changed, those two! Is he still beating her? Rusty's hair has really grown. Did she go away over the winter? When did I last see her? The grey man is more and more ill, his AIDS is depriving him of his eyes and to think that not so long ago … '

And then there are those encounters I will never forget. That very young man who began to cry at the sight of my dog, because the previous day he had had to get rid of his golden retriever. He was no longer strong enough to walk him. His illness, AIDS of course, didn't allow him to. His kindly friends had advised him not to keep the dog, for they knew how close death was, how hastened things became. He knew it as well. But he would have wanted to extend life and keep the joy of time, of pressing against the body of his dog, so alive, so warm. By her smell, by her fur, my dog, Sud, had reminded him of that separation. Physical death might be nothing more than the logical and almost heedless extension of that first abdication of the self. Several months later, not having crossed paths for some time with this man, I came across his photograph in the obituary column of the newspaper. That's how I learned that his name was Hervé. A funeral service would take place the following day at the church not far from us. We were asked to attend without any further form of invitation. The day of the funeral, I had neither the desire nor the courage to go to the ceremony. But the church bells rang long and hard and my dog greeted them with very loud barks.

Sometimes more sordid encounters come along and shatter the order of time into thousands of scattered pieces. For years, almost every morning I would run into an elderly, taciturn and unfriendly man, who begrudgingly walked a small dog, as capricious as a child. With time, I came to tame this man, and sometimes he would say hello. This said, I never managed to win over the little beast, whose growls, directed at both Sud and me, would get louder by the minute. Saturdays and Sundays this man was accompanied during his walks by his boyfriend, a man of the same age, the true owner of the dog. Through this man, who didn't hesitate to make contact, I learned that the dog despised females and that the last time he had been made to smell the ass of a bitch in heat, he had been sick for three days, vomiting. I understood that this man wanted to express something of his homosexuality, but I'm accustomed to neuroses and his words left me mostly indifferent.

One day it was very cold, and the father of the dog in question walked the dog in his arms and entered into the building crying out vigorously that he was going to heat up a nice comforting meal for Oscar. His lover held the door open for him to make room for the little dog. All of this man's moroseness was attached to the love his boyfriend bestowed on Oscar, and his obligation, every morning, to walk the dog he would otherwise have been quite happy to toss down the garbage chute. Soon, I no longer saw the taciturn man walk the little dog. Oscar's dad alone walked the little animal, who was visibly gaining weight. The dog only ever left its owner's arms to quickly pee. I thought the taciturn man had won; he had likely explained to his boyfriend that the dog was not his, and that if he wanted to act senile, he was welcome to do so, but alone. In addition, the dog's dad was transforming from one day to the next: he had changed his haircut, dressed carefully and was even more smiling than usual. 'There's nothing quite like leaving regression behind, I told myself. It's good for everyone.'

Several months later, when Olga and I were in the elevator with the little dog and his owner, the latter declared to us almost triumphantly, after the usual formalities: 'You know, my lover, whom you used to see with me in the elevator, well, he passed away three months ago.'

I hate the expression 'passed away.' Euphemisms get on my nerves and I have a hard time understanding that someone is dead when that idiom is slipped into a conversation. Nonetheless, I began immediately to cry, yelling and insulting all those around me. The absence of the taciturn man in the building where he should have been had he not been dead was unbearable and seemed so sad. The blasted little dog began to growl at me immediately. It was unacceptable to him that someone should cry for the man who had walked him for so many years. When he saw my tears, the little dog's owner said to me, 'But things like this happen. He had lung cancer, it's better this way, have a good day!' The elevator door had just opened. Death happens, of course, but when you live with someone for seventeen years (as I learned from the doorman), have the decency, at least, to treat him like a dog.

Sud is ill. I am writing down these words to contain the panic that seizes me when my dog is unwell. She vomited all night and her body has transformed itself into an immense rejection pump. The whole house bears the traces of her vomit that I follow, that I accompany faithfully. I clean, even if I'd rather be doing something else. I pretend to remain on the side of humanity, of sanity; I clean even while I hallucinate that I am rolling myself in all this vomit, dressing myself in it, that I am participating in this illness. I massage my dog's stomach, but she isn't well enough to accept my caresses. She turns around and around in the house in search of her normal body. She's doing poorly. We spend the night caught in the movement between life and death — at any rate, the death that I fear one day for her. I am afraid of the day when she dies, and unlike what I think of the death of my loved ones, I cannot even hope that Olga and I will die before her. Who would take care of her? Reason demands that she die before me. Reason commands me to witness that Sud is a dog, a carrion eater on the road to death, and I hope that she will know how to guide me, this dog to the blind person that I am.

In the morning, her stools are full of blood. I become bestial. Sud is not talking and I can't bring myself to speak for her. I become incoherent, my head full of cries. Of howls. That beat down on me. I become a dog, a wolf rather, captive, caught in the trap of death. With the years, my becoming-animal is more and more manifest. Sud has not become human, but me, I am a beast. And feral. I suffer without speaking. My dog will have saved me from hysteria. Before, I was unable to speak, my body manifested signs, tried to articulate things for me. Now, there is nothing but the cadaver's shit, blood and sufferings, which no longer signify anything. Meaning has fucked right off, it has come undone. I hope to die like a bitch. And these pages are nothing but a prosthesis in place of what meaning has been removed. An extensive comedy condemned to nothingness, or, worse, to some small vanity.

In the park, I met a remarkably ugly girl and her absolutely superb dog. James, the dog, is very skittish. He jumps at the slightest sound and wants to go home. Sud adores this dog whom she can dominate and beside whom she appears to exhibit exemplary courage. Two years of playing in the park and teasing him and James is moving away with his mistress. I meet her by chance at a book launch. I ask for news of James. 'I put him to sleep,' she answers in her mother tongue. The scene of the 'passed away' is played out for me once again. 'Why? You had him killed?' I shout into the ears of the poor girl. She switches back to French for fear that I will hit her: 'He was too fearful. He didn't have a good quality of life.' If we've reached the point of judging the quality of life of living beings, now, in order to allow ourselves to annihilate them, we are in danger of eliminating a good number. I think that this girl is very ugly, very very ugly. Like in a Jean Leloup song. And that her quality of life, which is most likely mediocre, must suffer as a result. I am called upon to see her often, she avoids me. She lives well with her guilt and her shame. But not with the words I throw at her face.

M y former students bring me down, they depress me, they poison my life and end up destroying me. I am decidedly not a good mother. I am the thankless mother. If I could, I would renounce them all with a single act of sacrilege. The other day, while I was crossing the street, three of them, whom I hadn't noticed, called out to me. They are, in all probability, quite happy to see me again. Not me. We are in front of the most highly esteemed anglophone university in North America, the university of rich anglophones and francophone upstarts who dream of forgetting their origins. My old students belong to the second category. I quickly determine that they are doing their Ph.D.s on seventeenth-century literature or on some Canadian woman author who spits all over Québec. They are studying there and they smile at me on the street, thinking it will make me happy to know that they, too, have taken to literature. They infiltrate my lineage, devour my descendants. They are proud to show me that they have followed in my footsteps, and as for me, I abhor them, I vomit them, I disown them, and far more than three times. I spent so many hours showing them that literature also meant not going to that university, I exhausted myself telling them to work on something other than Gabrielle Roy and the whole right-thinking non-committal literary institution, that I want nothing to do with them. I curse them. They keep me at the street corner to announce their thesis topics and to quote the names of their thesis supervisors, academic personalities I want nothing to do with. I feel nauseated. It takes hold of my stomach. It shakes spasms through my body. I taught in vain, and worse yet, they like to think of themselves as vague disciples of mine. They ask where I'm teaching and for how much longer. I tell them until I die. They'll go and repeat my witticism, thinking they will have discovered there some hidden meaning. Let them keep to their mediocre interpretations and let them become profs. I only wish them that at which they already excel: mediocrity at twenty-three.

Death shelters me from my students; when I meet one, I need only say that a friend died of AIDS to cut the insipid conversation short. The funereal protects me, the funereal produces the effect of a condom. I drape myself in my dead, I roll myself in a funeral shroud.

Literature taught my former students that it was necessary to speak of death through metaphor, and without the use of stylistic devices they start equivocating, they become disconcerted. Death: they are so afraid of it that they tame it early so as not to have to think about it when the time comes.

When a colleague from another university died, suddenly, as they say, of a heart attack, just as the department was in the process of selecting his replacement for the following year, the year of his retirement, people were somewhat disoriented. They had done well to think of replacing him (even if that may well have killed him), but no one had organized a conference or edited a special issue of a journal for him. He left too quickly, without homage, without one of his former students writing some insipid text on his exceptional teaching abilities in the thirties, when he was flirting with the far right. Since nothing had been prepared in advance, it was necessary to improvise, to organize both a conference and a special issue at the same time. With the greatest academic clamour. Since he hadn't accomplished much in his life (which I admired in him even if he had been senile and cruel for ten years), it wasn't so simple. The conference was entitled 'Surrounding Pierre Rochant' because it wouldn't have been easy to produce something on Pierre Rochant and his work. There would have been little to say. Since then, conferences are held in honour of the future dead three years before their retirement. Why not bury them here and now and right in front of their eyes? Why not mourn when there is nothing to mourn, celebrate our mediocrity immediately, because later, when the colleague is dead, we may no longer want to? What's more, an advance death provides the excuse not to think about it when it happens. 'It is mandatory for the professor to attend the conference held in his or her honour in order to kick the bucket' is what universities should write in their hiring contracts.

There are also those who die young — not those with AIDS or cancer, whom we can watch die progressively, little by little, and for whom there is time to organize plenty of events and pettinesses while remaining discreet. No, I'm talking about sudden deaths that subtract life from those who have not yet been prepared by the institution to leave. Those are the ones universities are crazy about. No guilt there for having done nothing before the death of said colleague. How could we have known? What's more, instead of throwing into question the meaning of life, on the contrary, these deaths, which are so absurd, so unthinkable, comfort the oldest among us who feel designated by some god for not having perished so young and for having had the time to complete task upon slavish task.

People like the death of young university professors: it provides the opportunity to sixty-year-old greybeards to teach a lesson, during a solemn ceremony, on the meaning of life – in other words, on the meaning of their own lives – and to quote Seneca on the brevity of earthly things. It provides the opportunity to feel sheltered and to think that youth moves too quickly and will get its just deserts. It provides the opportunity to speak of the immaturity of the work of the young deceased colleague, of the notoriety and glory he would have known had he been able to live a little longer. It gives the overall impression of having lived all these years solely to write three or four totally pathetic theoretical books, and it provides a raison d'être for their decrepitude, what they call being chosen. Yet what's saddest of all is that these young dead have already written books and articles of the highest importance, and they have been ignored with the idea, sustained by the mediocre living, that the œuvre was yet to come. The jealousy of those old professors is such that they speak, during the elegy, of fragments of thoughts and of a work in progress. 'If only he had lived … ' The annihilation of the generations that follow, their reduction to silence, to death, their erasure from memory: everything is set in motion for the embalming of the species. And we look through the biography of the young colleague for moments when he might have had some premonition of his sudden death. In such and such a year he spoke of this, in such and such year he did that: he knew death was lurking. And those of us who feel nothing, we professors who happily participate in the baseness of the institution, we, old fools that we are, who attach ourselves to life while riveting ourselves to common stupidity, since we haven't the slightest prescience of our own death, we will live to be at least a hundred years old, pushing our pens across pitiful sheets of paper, writing elegies for those who will have died at thirty, and we will put off catching up with them for as long as possible.

During one of these many ceremonies, in memory of a young woman professor, dead at twenty-nine, mangled in a car accident, I took note of the narrative air the older colleagues took on. They were there, ready to tell the incredible death of their former colleague whose body had barely had time to cool, and to recite, with nostalgia, entire passages from poems they had learned in their youth, in high school. The husband of one of the colleagues confided to me that when his wife received the news by telephone during a visit overseas, she had such a devastated air about her that he thought, for a moment, that their country home had caught on fire. 'But no, Monsieur, it was nothing but the death of a twenty-nine-year-old colleague, and I don't understand why your wife had that burned-down-country-home look, for, on the contrary, she had just gained a task that would keep her busy for the following months and provide her with a reason to live.' In fact, the woman in question spoke at the ceremony to say how deeply this death affected her personally. What was most awful was that she was clearly truly sincere. For this woman, looking like her house had just burned down is surely proof of great pain, for what could be worse in her narrow existence than to have lost her house? Indeed, she recounted the anecdote all evening long, and not without a degree of pride.

At that same event there was also Bob, who didn't stop crying, to pay homage to the last one hired in his department, the dead woman. Bob was unable to say any more than the others – he too was caught in the trap of narrating his encounter with the deceased – but there was true helplessness in his voice, if only in the irony or in the evocation of the body of the dead woman and her charm. I want my words here to be like Bob's, cruel and stumbling, but before all else cruel and stumbling toward me, against myself. I want words that make me suffer when I speak of my dead, words that make me grind my teeth, that hurt, over and over again, words that feel vain, words that betray. I refuse anaesthetizing words. Words that console, forgive.

Bob read his speech to the end, without batting an eye, and the following morning he signed a letter of resignation from his position as department head of sociology. He later explained to me that the work of director had become unbearable. He had the impression that he had been appointed solely to hire this young brilliant intellectual and to be there at the moment of her death in order to ensure that something appropriate be said about her. His task ended there, he was done with that piece of destiny.

Burying the dead, being there to witness, to pay homage, to receive messages from beyond: there are people who also exist simply to carry out those tasks.

There are the dead who haunt you and don't leave you alone, those who follow your every step, who manage even to take your place in daily life, those who erase you from events in favour of their existence: they are ghosts, parasites, bloodsuckers from the beyond, who demand reparation or, worse, some vague revenge. That's the category into which I would put Hamlet's father, for example. And then there are the dead who make themselves discreet, who send messages but not too often, who remain hermetic and distant and who sometimes shed doubt on the existence of the beyond, then provide reassurance several days later, but never unequivocally. Those dead must be invoked, called up by seers, invited to a round-table discussion, be made to appear in dreams: they need a channel of communication. And the frequency of the common channel is then full of interference. My dead play hide-and-seek with me. They appear only to disappear and there they are again later, but in another form that I am unable to understand. Which explains my passion for signs and interpretation. I look for the dead in every fold of my life and I don't want to miss the moment when they will manifest themselves. I have antennae everywhere.

My grandmother appeared to my father on the eve of my birth, and ever since I have been wrestling with the beyond. I live under the sign of apparitions, and of disappearances especially. When I was small and we would go to Europe, my mother would take me with her to place flowers on the graves of all the deceased from the past, all those I never knew but to whom I owed so much. As if the family of the dead weren't big enough as it was. I had to visit all the cemeteries of Canadian, British and American soldiers who lie in Norman earth. Not to mention the grave of the unknown soldier or the tombs in Parisian cemeteries that I visited to pay homage to Piaf or Musset. I know all of France's and Navarre's cemeteries. My mother was so unhappy living in North America. It wasn't the land of her dead. Of American cemeteries I knew nothing, except for military cemeteries, in particular that of Arlington, near Washington. In my mother's eyes, American soldiers fought for the liberation of France and are therefore our family, our very own dead.

My mother's passion for cemeteries is at the heart of my urban and personal geography. For a long time I lived opposite cemeteries without realizing it, and even when I went to live for several years in Europe, I found myself near the American cemetery in Suresnes. In the vicinity of a cemetery, I find my bearings easily; far from cemeteries, I am a bit disoriented. Now, I live far from the dead. I find it more practical to carry them with me. Intermittently. I invented the portable dead.

And then my mother's other passion is for photographs of flowering graves. Entire albums are devoted to this genre. Great-Aunt Louise's grave was better flowered than Great-Aunt Suzanne's — the comparative study is very well documented. My mother, who hasn't set foot in France for over twenty-five years, is neglecting all of her duties and no longer honours her dead. Nonetheless, she is still capable of appraising their graves.

When my grandmother died by chance in Québec, during a visit to see the family, her body had to be repatriated to France. It wouldn't have occurred to the family to proceed otherwise. My grandmother therefore left once again for France, but in a special coffin designed to not transport indigenous diseases. Hermetically sealed with lead. So my grandmother is buried like an American soldier, on the Norman coast, facing the Atlantic Ocean, which continues to separate us from her, although differently.

When my cousin, who joined the French army out of loyalty to his origins, even though he had spent his whole life in Montréal, died in Europe during a military exercise, his family, who had long ago immigrated to Québec, had his body repatriated 'to North America,' which, by this fact, became my own homeland. Homeland, soldiers, mean almost nothing to me, and yet ... The first dead of the second generation had to die on French soil and be repatriated here, home. The first dead had to be a soldier and I continue here on North American soil to flower military graves.

In our family, cadavers cross the ocean; death is transatlantic, and I cannot take an airplane to Paris or Barcelona without a certain shiver. I think sometimes that I will die mid-flight, in the very middle of the ocean, so as not to have to choose the place of my burial, or else I imagine my ashes scattered in the cold waves of the ocean from atop some giant liner, like the one my mother took the first time she touched upon Québec. In our lives, our birthplace is of little importance. It's the search for our place of death that keeps us going.

Apparently, due to continental drift, the Atlantic Ocean is growing day by day, month by month, year by year. This geographical imperative fills me with dread.

My mother's aunts, my great-aunts, were also passionate about tombs. I suppose that's where my art comes from today. From time to time they would go and pay a visit to their dead husbands and busy themselves ordering what would sooner or later constitute their little 'home.' Have the angels repainted gold, the inscriptions re-engraved and, most of all, ensure that no one from the family has had the audacity to take one of their places inside the crypt – such were their primary tasks. The little fairies of death who were once my great-aunts are now dead. They are quietly tucked in, practically by themselves, in their crypt, the family drawer. Since their deaths, the cemeteries are a little more unkempt and the family a little less impeccable.

Graves are not limited to cemeteries; apparently the threshold of Gainsbourg's old building is strewn with flowers. Paris is an immense cemetery, but it's true of every city, every village, of the world. The world is haunted.

My other grandmother, on my father's side, is buried facing the Mediterranean, in Muslim earth, although in the Christian enclave of the cemetery. They are my other dead, not my oceanic nor my military dead, but my Southern dead, my dead in hot ashes, my dead from where it's good to be alive. I know these dead less well. On my father's side, there is a tendency toward superstition, and people don't speak of death. It brings on the evil eye, as well as black cats, black curtains, black in general. Needless to say what colour I wore as a teenager, nor to describe my relationship to my father. At home, black is not the colour of mourning, it's rather that of provocation. Provocative black. Black provokes evil. When I am in mourning, I do not wear black; at such times, I am in mourning for the colour black.

To write of the dead, because we leave them nothing of themselves, because they leave with nothing of us, to write against their very bodies, in order to mark them. My dead, do you still speak of me?

There was Hervé whom I loved and who died of AIDS, he, too, without my knowledge, without my understanding. Hervé was my hairdresser, even if I couldn't really afford to have my hair cut at such extravagant prices. He generally cut the hair of chic men and women and of the most fashionable models. And yet, every five weeks, I entered that posh salon to have my head tidied up. Hervé spoke little, he cut my hair conscientiously and I scrutinized each of his gestures as if through a magnifying glass; I was trying to glean information about him, I listened to what the other hairdressers said, the battery of assistants, the five receptionists. Little was said. Hervé was discreet, very discreet. One day someone wished him a happy birthday weekend, from which I was able to deduce that he was born on the 1st or 2nd of November. On All Saints' Day, of course. From then on, I believed us predestined for one another; I was also born on the Day of the Dead and imagined between us a shared sensibility. But the truth of it was I never knew.

When I saw Hervé's photo in a women's magazine that was paying homage to him (since he was dead), I was seized by a violent fit of tears. One evening, Matt, that little bitch, who cut the hair of women who were just as bitchy, confided to me that Hervé was ill. 'He has something between indigestion and gastroenteritis,' the little bitch whispered in my ear, because the music at the bar forced me into this

65

unpleasant contact. So I didn't understand that Hervé was at death's door. A week later, I saw Matt once again at the grocery store and in response to my question he gave me news of Hervé, saying that he wasn't doing any worse, 'but we still don't know what it is.' Matt switched to English, his mother tongue, in order to convince me of the truth of his utterance. At that precise moment, his change of language allowed him to see himself as a good person, someone who holds his tongue and doesn't spread offensive rumours about the health of his friend Hervé. The change to English and the profound air he adopted gave him the illusion of carrying the secret of the gods and of not betraying Hervé. For months that little bitch, Matt, must have taken great pride in his silence surrounding the gravity of Hervé's illness, to the point of forgetting his own glory, because that little cretin doesn't have enough of a brain to remember his acts of bravery over a span greater than six months. But I remembered the change to English and the knowing look Matt assumed at the grocery store, and was only able to decode them much later, when, after Hervé's death, I sought to understand why and how I had never known anything about his AIDS. And yet God knows the degree to which AIDS inhabits me and that I suspect all the healthy people of the world of hiding their illness from me. For me the entire universe is in a terminal phase, but for that particular Hervé, I saw nothing, nothing until his photograph in the April 1993 issue of *Elle Québec*. I didn't get it. And I can't even blame it on the little bitch, Matt. I never knew a thing and I certainly never understood. I wanted so badly to keep Hervé with me, in this life, I admired him so, and in my eyes he embodied every possible quality, all the graces of the living, so that I couldn't even think that he was sick. And yet, shortly after a Christmas Eve party, breaking his usual silence, had he not told me, while cutting my hair with his nimble fingers, that he had been very ill on Christmas night? He had brought his parents, who lived in London at the time, a semi-preserve of foie gras, and after the collective sampling, he had been the only one in the assembly to be poisoned by the food. He ended up in hospital and finished 'Christmas on his back' as he told me laughingly. 'I have a fragile immune system,' he added so that I would understand. But I understood nothing and yet I recorded his words in my very entrails. They echo through me now horrifyingly. How could I have retained those words, preserved them and not decoded them? Is that the meaning the story of the semi-preserve holds for me? Sibylline, suggested words whose true meaning escapes me, preserved for later, when I would be able to understand them, powerlessly. Semi-preserve which will poison me forever.

So, Hervé told me much and I understood nothing. I contented myself with recording. I was an automatic answering machine and nothing more for him. He left his voice on the admirable machine that I was, and I listened to the message only too late. The night on which I read of his death and saw his photograph, Hervé appeared to me in a dream. Some would say prosaicly that I dreamt of him, but to those I would answer that dreaming of Hervé is nothing new for me and that on that night, he appeared to me, for he was not alive in my dream, but very much dead. He had come to say goodbye to me and to apologize for not having done so sooner. The thoughtfulness of his gesture indicated to me right away that it was Hervé's ghost. He took me into his arms, held me very hard, and I was suddenly panic-stricken: 'But who will look after my hair now?' and he answered kindly, as he was wont to do: 'And me, who looked after my cadaver's hair?' And since I didn't know how to answer, he smiled and said, 'It's okay, the hair of the dead is of no importance.' And he left.

Since Hervé's death, my hair no longer holds the same importance. I am not yet in the world of the dead and it does preoccupy me somewhat, but it's not the same anymore. I'll have my hair cut anywhere, without anticipation, without ritual. Nice and quickly. And yet Matt, that bitch, who cuts my cousin's hair, tried to become my Hervé. He had the audacity to say that now that Hervé's no longer around, he hoped to have me as his client. The bastard sees himself as the heir to all the heads groomed by Hervé. But I won't ever go and have my head touched by him. I know he was a friend of Hervé's, but what he might tell me about the latter in English in order to be more convincing, I can say without even having heard it spoken. Matt is incapable of saying anything interesting; that's the way it is. Everything in him is a clutter of clichés.

Now, I walk around with my tangle of hair, my mad hair, my half-dead hair, and when I see Matt, I pretend not to noticed how incensed he is by my messy head, my striped roots and my excessively discoloured ends. Matt looks at me with a proprietary air; slowly but surely, I will succeed in demolishing this commodity, my body. Apparently, Hervé would have bequeathed him my head and he threatens to sue me one day for damages. Sometimes he wishes for my death because he finds it indecent that I exist and take such little care of his possessions.

He doesn't understand why I didn't follow the example of all those women who passed over from Hervé to him without even noticing the difference.

My hair belonged to Hervé, and since his death its value has doubled on the hair market. I am not just anybody: I used to have my hair done by Hervé, and whoever takes over definitively can claim victory. Hairdressers fight over my hair, and as for me, I persist in doing my hair less and less well and in changing hairdos with each cut. This is how I remain loyal. And in my hair, rebellious.

I am awoken at nine a.m. by my mother's voice on the answering machine. Her voice weeps, my half-brother died in the night. Heart attack in his sleep. How does one mourn a brother one hardly knew, the son one hasn't seen in over twenty-five years? How is one to mourn what was experienced as dead all this time? I know the cruelty of my words and the horror they provoke in me. Our cruelty is what will kill us, our inhumanity. I observe that I am becoming inhumane. This observation is all the humanity I have left. My half-brother, Patrick, will be buried on the other side of the Atlantic, in Europe. He always rejected the family's immigration. He will be buried in his country. But not one of his brothers or sisters will set flowers on his grave. No one will attend his funeral. He is only a half-brother, a half-son, and has been half-alive, and fractionally dead to us for so long. Europe is too far; the Atlantic grows wider each day, time passes from second to second and, here, we forget those who live and die over there, just as they forget us. At least I hope so for their sake.

How many more dead before the end of this book? How many telephone calls, secret alarms and peals of destiny? And then the question of the end of the book, of the unexpected end, the possible death of the author, which I am not positing, but it's there, in every one of my words, in every one of my dead.

Hervé died in his sleep as well, but he was much younger than my half-brother, even if he remained a half-friend. Hervé was a lawyer, already famous by the time he died at twenty-three. A go-getter, the son of an immensely rich magistrate. But since a lawyer's career was insufficient to feed Hervé's enormous appetite for living, he also studied Slavic literature with me, and with the most feverish loyalty. I liked this boy whom I had seen hanging out in the bars several years earlier, when he bore a vague resemblance to Mick Jagger. When I saw Hervé again in my class, I told him how he had appeared to me at sixteen. He seemed stunned to learn that a perfect stranger knew so much about him, when he knew nothing about me and didn't even remember my face. I have an extensive memory.

I am a giant closet in which the past accumulates. In this way, without intending to, I dispossess people of their history, which I keep inside of me. It's what Providence gave me and it isn't easy to be alone with the past. I would even go so far as to call it my curse. After having shared a laugh with me about my espionage of his adolescence, Hervé became a friend with whom I had long discussions after seminars, about everything and nothing, about Dostoevsky, Raskolnikov, crimes, punishments, and the best hash in town.

We weren't friends. Hervé ran untiringly from every situation. Run for your life ... A lawyer, Hervé wanted to teach literature, but when he spoke to me, he was always looking at his watch so as to be on time for the courts or some meeting he couldn't afford to miss.

He thought I was chasing after him, that I liked to see him run; I forced myself to court him gently, just so I could watch him escape so elegantly. One day, unable to take much more and in order to protect himself from a potential attack, he made me understand that he had a girlfriend. I pretended not to hear, not to understand, just for the pleasure of seeing him take to his heels and attempt to escape. I am sure that with his girlfriend, Christine, he sometimes spoke of me or of another. Nowhere to be found. That's where Hervé was. Always somewhere else, with the passion for in-betweenness in his gut, the rage of escape. He died at twenty-three, May 9th, in his sleep. I don't know his birthdate, but I know the date of his death. In the obituary column, his parents published a photo in which he holds his lawyer's degree in one hand. Hervé was found in his bed, dead in the small hours of the morning. That's no destiny. Four insidious deaths in the night, four unannounced deaths, is simply not a normal statistic in the life of every forty-year-old. I have to find some reasonable order in among all of this.

I told many friends in literature of Hervé's death, and since no one knew the name of this boy who wasn't very present, always between two doors, I thought perhaps that Hervé had only existed in my imagination, until the day I announced the news to Angela, who said, 'You don't mean that magnificent boy with whom you often had long discussions and who paralyzed us all with his beauty?' It's true that

Hervé was beautiful, it's true that he was gorgeous, and I don't know by what movement of modesty or reserve I had never stopped to think about it. I tried out my new strategy for announcing Hervé's death on other literature colleagues: 'You know that gorgeous guy who was in our classes, well, he's dead!' And I must admit that my interlocutors knew immediately whom I was talking about. I find it ironic to speak of Hervé in this way, but I quickly realized that to continue to evoke the beauty, which haunts us still, of someone who has died, is a lovely way to pay homage. Such is my punishment for having refused to see it sooner.

I hope Hervé accepts the beyond. He who had such a passion for in-betweenness, I hope that he has not remained between life and death, in the kingdom of the undecided, in the world of limbo. With the anger of dying. It must be awful to remain in that in-between place. But, beautiful boy that Hervé was, he will always escape to where he wants: all the doors of heaven and hell will remain forever open to him.

There are people whom we absolutely don't want to see die before us, because they are people we despise. Since there is a theory that suggests that someone from the beyond will come and collect us here below, I prefer that my enemies remain alive, for I have no desire to see their radiant faces when I pass through to the other side. Let them rejoice, but in the world of the living, there is at least a chance I won't see them.

I recently learned, while watching television, that a journalist who interviewed me at length last year on the subject of AIDS came within a hair's breadth of death. During his long coma, of course, he split off from himself (as is minutely described in personal accounts) and encountered all the dead of his life, who came to talk to him and explain that he must follow them. This counsel from the family of the dead is fascinating. I often wonder who will be there when I die, the makeup of the council being nonetheless subject to fluctuations, since it will all depend on who dies before me and, as such, on the moment of my death. At the expanded family council of the dead, there may be more or less of a crowd, a larger or smaller number of guests, and I wonder if there are any dead who will abstain from showing up, who will snub us or refuse us entry, if the authors on whom I will have spent my life working will come and collect me or not, even if I never knew them when they were alive. These are very practical questions to which, more often than not, one becomes attached. I have the feeling that Hervé will not come, that he will refuse to come and greet me. There will, of course, be no shortage of Hervés, but there will be one, at least, who will boycott me, who will spoil my party.

Angela, who is a veritable encyclopedia of thanatology, thinks that on the other side, over there, where the dead are, the place that I am incapable of naming, they are grouped into cells. There would be the Marx cell, of that Angela is certain. In this cell, one works for humanity according to rules unknown to, and particularly misunderstood by, the living. People gather from time to time to know what is required in order to continue the struggle and one is selected from among the living, the chosen worker of the month. This theory enables Angela to explain Deleuze's suicide. Marx's cell would have held a family council meeting and decided that he was needed up there. I quite like the idea of being grouped together according to intellectual affinity. I don't know if it's possible to be in two cells at once: Marx's cell, for example, and Freud's as well. On this subject, Angela tells me that one doesn't choose her cell and that anyway, up there, Freud has submitted to Marx for the good of humanity. What horrifies me is that, inside these cells, we find ourselves with creatures we've spent our lives abhorring. We learn tolerance, for the good of humanity and Marxist thought. It's a little like the land of the living, only worse.

Angela sometimes forbids me to speak ill of Claire, because she believes her colleague will be a member of the

Marx cell. And since I too will be a member of that cell, confirms Angela, I am called upon to put up with Claire for eternity, uncomplainingly. All the more reason to speak ill of her while I'm alive, no?

Carla is an Argentinian friend whom I haven't seen for years. I know that she's in Montréal these days. I saw her name in a newspaper, she's giving a conference. I won't go and see her. The last time we saw one another, she bid me farewell telling me that we wouldn't see one another again in this world, but in the cosmos. And I don't want to break her promise. It's up to her to do it. I don't know why she spoke those words, but I respect them. Stupidly. Like some hope for a future life. 'Let's not make projects for this life-time, but for the next – there, we will have time,' that is if the cell theory is false, otherwise we will be too occupied. Carla always seems very busy and it's perhaps through meetings in the cosmos that she exonerates herself for not having enough time for us here below. It should be said that this girl brushes against death continually. The minute she boards an airplane there is a technical problem with the machine. One day, the airplane loses its radar over the Andes Mountains, the next day the landing gear doesn't work. Carla should be included in airline statistics, but statistics are not always well done. Her Argentinian friends who know about her aero-nautic powers despair and tremble when they see her climb into the same airplane as they. Carla brags about knowing before everyone else that the airplane has a problem. She recognizes it by its sound. She should be a mechanic. She is a professor of theology. Her sister was assassinated by the military junta in Argentina. This sister was a union lawyer and her body was found in a garbage bin. Carla jumps at the slightest sound of a siren. Her mother was not permitted to see the body of her dead daughter, because the family feared the reaction of a mother discovering the dead, tortured body of her child. So the mother entrusted Carla with the task of dressing the dead daughter, but Carla was unable to do so, and she didn't know how to tell her mother. She hadn't been able to touch her sister's mutilated body and fainted at the morgue. The mother dreamt that her dead daughter told her she was cold in her coffin. This is how she understood that Carla had lied to her and that she had never dressed her sister. She will never forgive Carla. The latter never admitted anything to her mother and never will. She left Argentina and returned alone to visit her sister's grave ten years after the funeral. One day, as I was speaking favourably of an Argentinian woman who had come to Québec to give a very militant, engaged talk, Carla said to me laconically, 'That Lupe was department head under the dictatorship, so you can imagine how engaged she is.' Carla will hate me for telling her life story poorly and quickly. You will be angry, Carla, and I hope you will make me pay for it in the cosmos, or better yet, sooner.

What I most despise about men, gay or straight, is their sexual identity. I could say, and it would be more simple, that I don't like men, but it isn't at all true. I don't even think bisexuality is the solution, that we are mixed into the Great Whole. But nothing disgusts me more than a group of fags laughing at a girl who's trying to pick them up, saying simperingly, 'if she only knew ... ' If she only knew what? That identity protects from everything?

Mike, a gay man who self-identifies as a 'butch-identified gay male,' confides in me, after a tutorial in which we have just met, that francophone women give him the eye and that they don't seem to pick up on his unmistakable homosexuality, which is so self-evident in his culture. He must think that I'm trying to pick him up and that I don't understand his raison d'être. So I pretend not to understand and continue to flirt with him, which really means that I do nothing other than listen to him without answering, which must be a sure sign for recognizing a straight woman. What could I say to reassure him? That I'm 100% lesbian? That I live with a woman that I must brandish every day like a standard? Would that stop me from falling madly in love with handsome Mike?

Since he must be reading my thoughts, which speak of mad love for him, he ditches me without the slightest explanation to go and kiss a boyfriend. There's nothing quite like a practical application of the truth.

Several months later, now that all the university gossip must have put him in the know and revealed to him the truth, the real truth, Mike rushes at me to give me a kiss. He mumbles something incomprehensible. I answer him coldly. It's too late. What might we become? Great friends certain never to desire one another? Accomplices whose well-delineated territories lie beyond or outside the realm of seduction? I'd rather never see anyone at all.

Angela, my friend here below, who is really my friend from beyond, is in love with Alberto, a magnificent boy, who swears only by men. Alberto often speaks to her of an American HIV-positive lover for whom he worries incessantly, and Angela knows that by telling Bill's life, Alberto is confiding his own condition. She will never tell him what she knows and Alberto will never admit the truth, because in his own way, he has already told. 'When we're similarly ill, then we can stand in judgement of that silence,' Angela often repeats to me. There are thousands of ways to tell and to be understood. In that half-silence, half-avowal, Alberto certainly offers Angela his deepest anguish, to which she otherwise wouldn't have access. Between them a thousand seductions, but especially that of death.

Alberto is absolutely jealous of all of Angela's lovers, whom he wants to meet when he passes through Buffalo. As soon as he meets them, he gives them the eye and tries to pick them up. Through this competition, Angela and Alberto are lovers by proxy. That, at any rate, is what I believe to be true. Mental safe sex, which may lead Angela to catch Alberto's virus without getting it from him directly.

When I met Olga, or rather the first time I kissed her, I dreamt that I had given her the AIDS virus and that her body and mine were covered in Kaposi. We had enflamed the illness into one another. Gloria, a very militant friend, asserts that lesbians don't share the same imaginative space as gay men. The relationship to the body, to death, is different. I am far from convinced.

AIDS hit Olga and me headlong. One way or another. We have so many dead friends. Lesbians aren't affected by AIDS. Really? On television, the wonderful doctor Willy Rozenbaum explained a number of years ago that people reproached him for his survival, that his friends, his patients, repeated to him ceaselessly, 'But you, you're still here to talk about it.' Furious, Rozenbaum answers simply that surviving people is also a hardship. It isn't so easy to care for people and watch them die. It isn't so easy to bury one's friends. There's no comparison between the living and the dead. Of course. But we each have our cross to bear. We each carry our share of fatality.

I am on my way home from Washington with Olga. Mandatory stop in New York. Into the airplane climbs Hervé, Olga's department head, and by the most unlikely chance, he naturally takes the seat behind hers. That's where the airline company put him. Quite simply. One year ago to the day, Olga and I were supposed to participate in a conference in Chicago where we were to meet Hervé, but I fell ill just before the plane took off. We had a year to change our tickets before their expiry, so we decided to go to Washington to see the Quilt Memorial, in memory of those who died of AIDS. On the way back from our pilgrimage, here we are then with Hervé behind our seats, when we should have seen him in Chicago, a year ago to the day. Pure coincidence? Maybe. Add the fact that our flight number is the same as that of an airplane that crashed over two years ago, carrying Olga's old department head, whom Hervé replaced at the university. In seeing Hervé arrive and sit down behind us, I am overcome with panic. I am afraid the plane will crash. Quite simply. It would be nothing more than pure coincidence. After all, what do all these coincidences mean? In Lisbon, Flavia, a colleague from Hervé and Olga's department, in whom Olga confided her terror of taking a plane again after the death of the old department head, claimed that it was impossible, according to all laws of probability, for two people from the same department to die in an airplane.

Olga and Hervé today, plus Olga's old department head, that would make two at once, bringing the total to three. Is that possible, statistically? As for Flavia's remarks, I found them completely ridiculous. What protection do statistics offer against death? Nonetheless, I repeat these words to myself throughout the whole flight during which Hervé is sitting in the airplane behind us, comfortably reading his paper. After the succcssful landing, I want to tell Hervé about my fear. But since I hardly know him, I'm afraid he won't understand. For him, this may amount to nothing more than pure coincidence. Does he see that he has taken the place, at the university, of another, of a dead man, a friend of his? Does he dare admit it to himself? And what does this interpretation amount to, anyway? Since we don't have the same view of the problem, we surely don't analyze the situation in the same way. As for me, I know that destiny has shown me its cards to make a mockery of me and that Jason, the dead department head, is winking at us from the beyond; I also know that we will hear from him again and that this series of coincidences will inevitably lead to further coincidences whose meaning will then become clear.

I have a dream in which I explain all of this to Hervé. He doesn't understand a thing, he cannot understand a thing, but he smiles at me.

I have just read the unbelievable and strange story of a mummy discovered somewhere in South America. The body is of a young girl who would have been presented as an offering to the gods. This body, offered up from the depths of time, has remained intact, or, at any rate, it is possible to distinguish the distinct likeness of a young girl through the features of the mummy. A shrivelled-up young girl, but she remains nonetheless. A face still among us.

There is something horribly magnificent about being killed at fifteen or twenty years old, about never having had the right to time on earth and about still being among us and among those who come after. A very close friend used to say to me, 'We need children because soon there will remain nothing of us. Nothing at all. We are condemned to the void.' In a way, my mummy offers herself up as an answer to my friend. What remains or will remain of us, no one can claim to know. And the intact body of this young sacrificed girl has me convinced of the reign of absolute arbitrariness when it comes to the history of our remains. Hervé Guibert hesitates all through his last books on what to do with his future dead body. Must he order the construction of a mausoleum and prescribe the positioning of his body in one place or another? Feet facing south, head facing east? And then sometimes he takes pleasure in imagining requesting that his body be placed in a bag and the whole thing tossed into the first available garbage bin. I believe now that his remains are somewhere on the island of Elba, a place he found such pleasure in visiting. But I may have invented that.

In a film by Greenaway, we see those drowned in the Seine during the Revolution. The film is a series of cadavers extracted from the water that the director resuscitates and buries with a single gesture. These people have been long forgotten and their death doesn't frighten us because, regardless, drowned or not, they would be dead now anyway. The passing of time enables us to tame our dead. And maybe they too are accustomed to death. Something of the erasure, of whiteness, is exposed in this film. These dead people, these dramas, these names that are no longer of concern to us, don't speak to us anymore. All that remains of them is the space of this little film. In black and white.

I don't know what to think. Of us, there remains little, and very quickly History buries us, condemns us to oblivion. Two or three names of people from the past become monuments to the dead for all the unknown soldiers of life. Two or three names, standard-bearers for the nation of the dead.

Camille. The name is inscribed in all of my mother's hats. Camille was the name of a fashion designer who died thirty years ago. But in my mother's unfashionable and precious hats, her name endures, and it's Camille whom my mother proudly continues to wear.

I remember almost nothing of Camille. She was a corpulent woman, very beautiful, Brazilian, who had two daughters, both a little older than me. With each new hat my mother tried on, Camille pulled her aside and made her promise to ensure that in her coffin she would be wearing her magnificent mauve dress. My mother would tell her to stop being so stupid. And Camille would laugh, she was always laughing. And she managed to make my mother promise. Camille was all joie de vivre. What a stupid expression, but Camille wanted people to believe in her stupidity. And people in her entourage had difficulty understanding her obsession with death.

One morning, Camille's assistant called my mother to tell her that Camille was dead, that she had committed suicide. Quite simply by putting her head inside a plastic bag. Smothered to death. I wondered throughout my childhood how she had found the necessary determination not to withdraw her head from the bag. How one decided to remain until the end. Every night before going to bed, I held my breath as long as possible, to see if, like Camille, I too had the courage to see it through. But I always started breathing again. I wanted to be as strong as Camille, but I was never able. I was haunted by her mauve dress in the coffin. People say of her that she had a very young lover. But no one ever knew why she killed herself. One of her daughters died several years ago of an overdose. She too left young children behind. That's all I know. But this absence of weakness in the face of death, this absolute determination, seem entirely heroic to me. Right or wrong. And when, on the first of January last year, I learned of Hervé's suicide, I thought once again of those deaths that unsettle because of their courage.

Hervé committed suicide by hanging himself from his sports equipment. But it wasn't a matter of swinging from the end of a rope after having suddenly hurled himself from the bench that supported his weight, with a kick in the air. No, Hervé attached a rope to his torture device, roughly one metre from the ground. He placed his neck very cautiously into the rope's knot and gently placed his head on a pile of pillows. So as not to suffocate all at once. Then he began the long work toward death. It was a matter of dying slowly and with every second remembering to push aside more and more pillows so that the head remained suspended in the air, without suffering.

So all of Hervé's attention was focused for a very long time on losing consciousness, while remaining alert enough to push aside the pillows. All of this I know because before achieving his hanging, Hervé made many botched attempts and explained to us how he had approached it, while swearing, of course, never to do it again. When he told us about his various attempts, it was impossible for us not to feel his pride. He found himself ingenious and intelligent. There was in him, in his accounts, something that indicated to us that he wasn't just anybody. Of course, his lover, Jean, often stopped him from dying. He often caught him in the very middle of his long deadly process, and Hervé recounted that each time he was resuscitated, his first emotion was sadness. He said he was deeply depressed at the idea of having to find the courage to resume the strenuous and meticulous work that was his death. Don't go believing that Hervé was crazy, insensitive or unaware of danger. Jean often found him in the bathroom sobbing in the dark. The machine of death assembled with the pillows. How many times did Hervé cry before botching a suicide attempt? How much cowardice did he see in himself? How many tears did he cry before finding the courage? But this courage, once he found it, he held it to the end, despite us all. I cannot think of him without admiration. There are those among us who reproach ourselves for not having helped him. There are those who say that it was cowardly to relinquish living. There are also those who declare that it was inevitable. The truth is somewhere, in a place I cannot access. But through his suicide, Hervé has earned himself in my eyes a halo of prestige, and I know that's what he wanted. To prove to all of us that he was capable. Coming from him, the courage he must have drawn from his very tears seems grandiose to me. That, I won't take away from him. Death must have appeared so inaccessible to him and yet he achieved it. Through determination. To Hervé I lift my hat, or rather I lift my mother's hats, in which the name Camille shines and assembles all of my labourers of death.

Apparently, young people commit suicide a lot in Québec. There are ostensibly countries in the world where the children of immigrants are the ones who want to end it all. Here, the children of non-migrant parents make up the horrible statistics. Four people commit suicide in Québec every day. That's more deaths than in car accidents, and I'm not even talking about AIDS. People commit suicide a lot in these parts. More than elsewhere? More than yesterday? Less than tomorrow?

A friend of Olga's believes that our society has become infanticidal. Yves is right: We revel in the death of children, we speak of youth's bleak future, we can't get enough of pedophiles and child-killers and the end of all posterity. We are more and more seduced by the death of little ones, as though it were the only death still capable of moving us. 'There is no real death but a child's!' This, Mallarmé wrote in his *A Tomb for Anatole*, a crypt poem to his young dead son. 'Il n'est de mort qu'enfant' is what they want us to believe. Death and children are everywhere. In a recent film, in a book by a father overwhelmed by the death of his four-year-old daughter, in every newspaper.

It's as if the death of children were the only hardship of reality left to us. Infanticide, the only murderer, and children, the only victims who have every right to be so because we can accuse them of nothing. The spectacle of that death brings down the house.

The future, if indeed it does exist, resides in the inversion of generations, in the devouring of the future, in its immediate consumption. The future will be a child-eater or it simply will not be. And struggles for the rights of children won't stop it from happening. On the contrary, it's all part of the spectacle. The echoes of *Kindertotenlieder* will remain with us for quite some time.

Good Friday is my favourite day of the year. Day of the death of Christ, a grave day on which one listens knowingly to the *Saint Matthew Passion*, day of rain or shine on which the devil beats his wife, so goes the expression, announcing the coming of spring. It's the day of Zeffirelli's *Jesus of Nazareth* on television, it's the day on which I suffer from being a non-believer.

Good Friday is my day of mourning, true mourning; I mourn the woman I cannot be, I mourn my desire for a god. At the age of eight, I had my tonsils removed on a Good Friday. My mother insisted that it happen on another day. But my pediatrician, who died several months ago as I learned from the obituary column, plotted with me so that Good Friday would be the day of my rebirth. My mother feared that I would pull a Christ on her and depart this life at three o'clock in the afternoon in the glory of my child-hood purity. But my pediatrician was adamant I have the operation and I listened to him. Every day during the three weeks preceding my operation, my mother repeatedly told me that the doctor was wrong and that without a doubt I was going to die. It took an extraordinary force for me to stick to my decision. A life force, but also the perverse and childhood force governing the desire to end it all. Before my operation, I played double or nothing inside my head. If I die, my mother's right, but if I live, I will be rid of her fears, superstitions and suffocations. I was operated on the morning of Good Friday in the year of 1969, and though I survived both prophecy and curse, my mother died a bit for me on that day. And she didn't resurrect on any Easter Day.

There was surely a first dead man or woman, but death existed of course well before the people who were subjected to it. It was a condition of my existence and I spent my childhood saying to my mother, 'I'm going to die soon, you'll see, at twelve or thirteen; I won't make it beyond that number.' Where did the intuition of my own death come from? Where did I get those magical numbers that ruled my childhood? My mother didn't respond to my terrorism. I think she was often afraid of me and my suicidal or morbid ideas. I frightened my mother. I didn't die at the age of thirteen, and it didn't surprise me. I had already symbolically buried myself in the garden, under the balcony.

I placed several objects into a box and with the neighbourhood children I staged what I pompously referred to as my funeral. A small cross in my memory was planted among the earthworms, spiders and weeds. I often watered the area so that flowers would grow on my grave. I dreamt of chrysanthemums, daisies, orchids and giant sunflowers. In vain. Who did I bury in that false garden crypt? What commemoration did I offer all the kids in the neighbourhood? I never knew. But, as for my survival and the declaration of my death, my mother was no doubt far more troubled than I.

At my birth, there was asphyxiation. I swallowed the amniotic fluid and, instead of filling my lungs with air, I was drowning in my mother. The doctors saved me just in time by cleaning out my lungs.

There was the first week spent inside an oxygen tent, the bloodless colour of my skin. There was the indifference of my mother, who didn't come to pick me up when my week in hospital was up; there were innumerable fits of suffocation and innumerable fits of breathlessness. Without question, I have a hard time breathing. I suffocate, and the worst death for me remains death by asphyxiation. As a child, Olga also nearly died of suffocation. Young children who were much older than she, who was only two years old at the time, used to pull on the long woollen scarf she proudly wore. The children, divided into two camps, pulled on the ends of the scarf, but in opposite directions. Olga's schoolteacher saved my Olga from dying. Little Olga, all blue in the middle of the yard … My uncle who is a doctor confirms that I'm a bit retarded because of my original asphyxiation. What's funniest of all is that at the age of thirteen, while eating a candy in his presence, I choked on it and he didn't budge. My mother had to save my life that time and she harshly accused her brother of incompetence. Without my knowing it, I must have replayed the scene of my birth, and, on that occasion, no doctor saved me, but my mother instead, whom I managed to pull from her indifference.

I often imagine myself as a gluttonous baby, greedy for amniotic fluid, wanting at all costs to keep something of my mother. I was already suckling inside her womb.

I was already mourning the woman I would lose.

Before our dead we must be ravenous, we must be cannibals and swallow them whole or tear them apart with our voracious teeth. We must binge on our dead or they will devour us. There's no way around it, it's the law of the jungle and of mourning. With each new dead, I dream that I'm eating fish and black noodles cooked in squid ink. And the dead I don't swallow stay caught in my throat.

Before our dead, we must be starving, greedy, our hands wide open for more. Death condemns anorexia. Death is a banquet, what can I say. At the death of Hervé, who disappeared in an airplane, it had been necessary to drink all the wine he had made, smoke all the cigarettes he had bought himself in all the airports of the world. After the death of her mother, Angela's fridge was full of vine leaves stuffed with rice that her mother had sent her several days earlier. What to do with them?

She could but eat them with the purest culpability and the greatest delectation. Her mother's last vine leaves. Could she not eat them, let them rot, like her mother's dead body? Angela ate them at the same time as her tears, gluttonously, without sharing them at all. Rapacity of death.

Smells are the very opposite of food; they are the impossibility of mourning and we needn't have read Proust to know it. Hervé would always put conditioner in my hair, something that smelled of the synthetic reconstitution of several products meant to repair the 'irreparable damage' of hair dyes. As soon as I open a bottle of that conditioner, it brings Hervé back instantly. But not Hervé in the flesh. No, something more suave and anguished. Of Hervé, all that is left is his evanescence. This conditioner plunges me into the most intolerable melancholy until its scent has been replaced by the reassuring smell of cigarettes, which guards me against all the anti-smokers. I drown in the sadness and loss of Hervé absorbed into my hair. Every time, it's the same thing: there are days when the absence of Hervé, his splash in the void, become so unbearable to me that I rush at another brand of conditioner, which then reminds me of my deliberate desire to forget Hervé. There's no way around it. The other day I thought I had found the solution. I couldn't remain in the grip of this fleeting, floating smell that I wanted to possess and with my two hands tear to shreds. I grabbed the bottle of reconstituted smells and simply gulped down its contents. I swallowed it all gluttonously, violently, without missing a drop. It was the only way for me to satisfy my appetite for Hervé. I was sick and I vomited.

It didn't pass. For days I kept the taste of Hervé in my mouth. I burped or vomited Hervé every fifteen minutes.

And yet, with time, I think it was the right thing to do.

It allowed me to try to digest Hervé's death.

With Olga, of course, my desires are cannibalistic. We do eat animals and yet we adore them. One would have to eat animals while adoring them, while sacrificing them. But as Olga says, all this flesh whose origins escape us is indecent. It would be more logical to eat our own animals, those we raise, those we love. Barbarity exists in the lack of proximity to dead flesh. Like it or not. It's not that I'm enraptured by cannibalistic practices, not at all. But my disgust at our relationship to consumption is even stronger. In fact, if we didn't have such a hidden and illicit passion for dead flesh, we would eat more insects in the West. I'm not a vegetarian. I can't do it; in fact, I wonder how Western vegetarians mourn their dead. Maybe they don't at all? As is often the case here at home. The question of mourning has become superfluous, because we no longer attach ourselves to people. And then there are those who live as one lives elsewhere, who identify with other people, other individuals, so the dead can pass through them.

One day while walking with a cousin whom I adore, we run into an unsavoury character who was once a friend. At least that's what I thought. As she walked past him, Lisa launched him a booming hello, whereas I merely looked through him, as though he no longer existed, since he is now dead to me. Lisa asks me why I don't say hello to Hervé. I have to explain to her that I have been too much a friend of Hervé's to be able to greet him now, today. I cannot reasonably say hello to people who are dead to me without feeling like I'm going crazy. Lisa seems puzzled. I ask her, 'But do you say hello to all the people you've had arguments with?' And Lisa answers, 'I'm sixty years old and I've never been close enough to anyone to stop talking to them.'

I'm still in shock from that sentence. Must I add that Lisa doesn't like meat, but that with age she eats more and more of it? Without passion, without reason. Lisa has no reason to be in mourning. And yet her sixty years remain caught in her throat and every day she tries sadly to swallow them by eating pork chops which she thinks will give her several years' more energy. But it's her grief that she swallows. Sixty years of non-mourning and non-death requires a tiny effort of mastication.

Lisa spends three hours a day bodybuilding and eating grapefruit. 'It eats fat.' She consumes herself in a sense, mourns the past that has settled in her flesh, that dissolves before our very eyes. Thankfully, ritual guards against madness.

It's just like dieting and anorexia. It's often a matter of the impossibility of mourning or the imperative to mourn. Is it possible to be rid of the past embedded in me? How does one keep nothing of time? And where, inside ourselves, must we keep past time? These questions are obsessive and shape our bodies. Psychoanalysis is nothing less than a theory of the body.

When in love, at the beginning of the relationship, there is something indecent about eating in front of the beloved. How unseemly to eat anything other than the object of love. And we do. We consume. It's so obvious.

Hervé Guibert speaks of AIDS devouring him. Must we imagine AIDS in love?

After having slept with someone one would rather not have slept with, those with solid stomachs feel like puking; those, like me, whose stomachs are more fragile, puke for real.

Consumption leaves a rotten aftertaste. And flesh, as well, goes bad.

A friend of mine, who is ugly, very ugly, spends her time bragging about people with whom she's slept. Of course, she only ever manages to sleep with people of great beauty. In this way, Marilyn believes herself able to forget her own ugliness. But one must be really ugly to sleep with so many people of such beauty, because only those who have been well served by nature can allow themselves to sleep with Marilyn without feeling threatened by so much ugliness.

Only the beautiful people of this world can condescend to that. And when Marilyn reviews the smutty list of her conquests, it always makes me want to cry. If she were beautiful, she would conceal the names of the ugly people with whom she sleeps.

I am always the one crying very loudly at funerals; I should have been a hired mourner, and this book exists to turn my tears into words. Who will cry this loudly at my funeral? They would have to start practicing now.

Every day, I walk past the hair salon where Hervé used to work. After the salon has closed for the day, I look through the window at the chair in which Hervé used to have me sit, as though I were a little girl, his own. That empty chair isn't only Hervé's absence, it's my death as well, inscribed there, because I will never again return to that chair under the same conditions as before. That empty chair is Hervé sending me the sign of my own death, which will arrive sooner or later.

'Look at us, absent,' he says to me.

I went to an auction yesterday for the first time in my life. There was something magical about the possibility of extravagance. To fall in love with an object from the past, since yesterday's sale items were antiques. The past fascinates me and yet I'm nothing of a historian. But the past I love is that of old objects or archeological digs. I like the monuments and the city of Athens where I have, of course, never been. There is a snobbery in me around having a Greek name and never having set foot in Greece. Let Greece come to me if it so chooses. My name is a meaningless signifier. And it is not so easy to inhabit. However much the Hellenic association of my university considers me one of its girls, I enjoy cold-shouldering my father's country. My classes are full of students with Greek-sounding names who, enticed by my name, hope to find in me their mother country. With my students, I discover the possible proximity of family names. Those students whose names end in 'akis' always smile broadly at me, and I respond in kind, happily, I admit. I consider the 'akises' like cousins, and it's true that I look like some of them. But so as not to feel sorry for my fake-Greek fate, I tell myself that I never liked my origins and that I never will.

During the building of the Athens subway, innumerable discoveries were made, and as Claudio's mother, Narcissia, who lives in Greece, said to me, if we revealed everything we found while digging for the subway, we would never be able to build it and the city of Athens would remain forever overfull of its past. All work would cease and soon the city would become an immense archeological site. Which it already is. But Athens's wonders must remain hidden, because there's no stopping progress.

I strike myself as one of those subway builders, those buriers of ruins and secrets. They make Athens speak so as better to silence it. Every day I discover the past, my past, my history and the history of others, but I must bury this discovery, bury it even deeper in me. In my life, progress will be comprised of the exhumation and burial in the very depths of my past of the dead around whom I must remain silent in order to continue. I, too, am the Athens subway. I move forward across the holy land of history, but it's in the soil of the future that I tread. I advance with my hair in the wind. Full speed ahead, I charge, full tilt, I bury time. On the way, I catch sight of Pericles and all the other ghosts who gesture to me, who offer a hand. I push them away, deep into my memory. It's up to others to save them. As for me, I can only move forward.

In London, when they dig to repair a gas leak in the Underground, they will find a small piece of the letter Hervé wrote to me just before dying in a thousand pieces, shredded by a bomb. In Berlin, when they dig to set the foundations of a new building, they will come across the general quarters of Hess or one of Hitler's bunkers. It's a question of which past.

My French friend Hervé loved ancient Greece. He taught himself Greek, even though his father was an eminent philologist, specializing in classical Greek. Hervé, of course, despised progress and even the telephone made him crazy. And yet I think that if he were still alive, he would have enjoyed exchanging long missives by e-mail. I think that if he were still alive, we would have gone to Greece together, we could have argued about that and a thousand other subjects and I would not now be a locomotive for the Athens subway. But it's because of Hervé, of his death, that I have become what I am, and I thank him for it. Just as I would have thanked him for what I would have been if he were still alive.

He promised me he would die on the shores of the Ganges, and I can't read Duras's *The Vice-Consul* without thinking of him. He died in Paris, in hospital. Just like Michel Foucault, whose agony I read and reread in his biographies and in Hervé Guibert's novel, *To the Friend Who Did Not Save My Life*. It's the only way for me to understand something of Hervé's death, because to date no one has wanted to talk to me about it. The friend who saved nobody's life: that's me. And I hope that my dead friends love me enough to resent me. Resentment toward someone who abandoned you along the way. I didn't go into death with them. I remained on the road. One day, it will be my turn to write a dedication to the friend who won't have saved my life. Isn't that what friends are for?

Hervé had one passion other than his passion for Greece: that of looking at the genitals of male horses. He who couldn't be torn from his Greek books became all of a sudden conciliatory when I suggested we go visit a neighbouring farm. He then got lost contemplating stallions, and inevitably asked me if I had ever seen such a well-hung horse. Which required a detailed response. A yes or a no wasn't enough. I had to provide profuse details and substantiate my comparisons. One day, Hervé admitted that he was doing research on whether the Trojan horse had been a beautiful stallion. Greece and horses had found a point of convergence.

Today, Angela is very sad. She calls me in tears — at least that's a metaphorical way of putting it, because Angela is so hard on herself that she would never cry in front of me. She is in love with one of her students and it isn't the first time. The feeling may be mutual, but Angela doesn't know what to think of herself. Is it fate? Another student told her one day that there are two definitions of the word 'lesbian.' First, there is the traditional and banal definition of the woman who loves women, and then there is the much more interesting definition of the woman who loves young men. And in both cases, the model would be Sappho. Angela is therefore a lesbian and we are members of the same community, even if I believe that many lesbians in the classical category wouldn't accept this dual definition. Angela and I often have a good laugh about our shared community. But tonight everything is sad. Heavy. Yet another young man. Is it a curse? I tell her to lean toward the genetic hypothesis; if it works as a strategy for gay men, why not for women who like young men? The categories need to be reinvented, and I make her laugh by telling her that after her death, the gene of her preference will be found by doing an autopsy on her cadaver. As for me, I would rather the community be as big as possible — too bad for lesbians in both categories who are a little too narrow-minded.

I dreamt of a city in which there was a mountain of garbage and gangs of female rats. I dreamt of a yellow fetid city, in which the sun couldn't look itself in the face, I dreamt of decomposing women that I voluptuously unearthed. I sometimes have such bad dreams that my days are completely ruined because of them. I need simply to await the following morning, tomorrow bringing the possibility of another happy day. And it doesn't always work. I live at the mercy of my nights. Who sends me all of these bad dreams and how am I to rid myself of them? To whom can I consign them? I also dreamt that Proust was riding a velocipede along the Grands Boulevards and that people on the road called him a pedalling pansy.

My dreams are never premonitory; they are, for the most part, interpretations of the present. A way of taking apart what's happening to me. My premonitions catch me off guard, unanalyzed. They rivet me to myself, add a weight that's unfamiliar. They are truly a burden.

It is, of course, necessary for me to write that I don't have premonitory dreams so that my dead can turn me into a liar and make a mockery of me. Saturday night, I dream that I am on my way to a funeral with a group of friends. The coffin is enormous. The ceremony, very solemn. I wake up Sunday morning and tell Olga that we are going to learn of someone's death. And since Olga is sometimes afraid of my words, I reassure her by announcing, without really knowing why, that it won't be the death of someone close.

It's disgusting, but we take consolation in convincing ourselves that it won't touch us too closely.

Sure enough, two days later, I learn of the death of Piero, who died in his sleep the night I dreamt of the funeral.

I must finish this book. The dead speak to me too much these days. They have become talkative and it's my fault. I don't want to be their official communication channel.

I am not Soviet television.

The other night, friends of Olga's speak to me of Hervé, who killed himself roughly a year and a half ago. Hervé and I went to school together over twenty years ago and I must say frankly that I always despised him. I wasn't the only one who felt hatred toward him. When he entered the jampacked lecture hall, the three hundred students present would look at one another, vexed to see him there again, still alive. Hervé wasn't a punching bag. Far from it, but he had a sort of inverted charisma which meant that no one could stand him. Every aspect of his character excited hatred and I tried a thousand times to struggle against the feeling he awakened in me. In fact, I think Hervé loved to be hated. It gave his life meaning. It allowed him to despise others, to construct himself socially. A friend at the time confided that she was in love with him. That she had spoken with him at length and that he had impressed her. There are girls who like to be scorned and I know that, for certain men, humiliation is as good a seduction strategy as any other. Hervé spat cheerfully on human beings and particularly on girls he managed to lay by treating them like little bitches.

I had forgotten about the abject existence of Hervé when, several years later, I found myself working in the same building as he. We crossed paths from time to time, watching one another with distrust from the corner of an eye, until the day he spoke to me, asking if I recognized him.

I had the arrogance to display the contents of my memory and to call him by his name, whereas he, of course, didn't remember mine. Obliviousness is the only guard against certain people.

One would have to feign stupidity and superficiality. But I haven't such humility. Hervé took pride in my remembering and believed he was something to me, when in truth I remember the names of dogs I meet in the park. He briefly told me what he was doing, vomited on my theoretical interests and declared himself erudite – a designation to which I was not entitled. For him, I was a fashionable girl who would fade away, who prostituted herself for the theory of the day. He would be a monument to the century. The erection of his era. He had just written a novel and so identified with Balzac, whom he admired more than anything, and he was preparing an enormous thesis, incomparable to the piece of shit I had just defended some five years earlier. That is how Hervé spoke to me, and I hoped that after all the insults he threw at me and the contempt he displayed he would never talk to me again. I was mistaken. He found my telephone number and decided to invite me over. I declined his invitations and made him understand that I couldn't stomach him. He mounted a conspiracy against me in the building that housed both of our newspapers, but his words found little resonance among his colleagues. One day in a bar, he came and sat at the table next to mine, where I sat with friends, didn't say hello and listened to my whole conversation while snickering. I pretended not to see him and indicated to my friends that they should follow my example. I never heard from him again. I learned that he called me a dirty dyke, and in that regard, he was entirely right. I learned of his death from people who detested him as much as I did. It's difficult to announce the death of someone you despise, and Hervé's death proved particularly difficult to announce. I have said so much bad about him, and if he were still alive, I would continue to do so. Of that, I am certain. It's difficult to hide the conscious joy his death brings. Yet each time I mention his name, people's eyes light up with joy, but also distress at feeling this joy. I could always not talk about that. I should probably proclaim that death erases everything and brings us peace with the dead. But Hervé's suicide proves the opposite. Of course, the fact that he committed suicide doesn't help: we all feel guilty for his death, guilty for having despised him, but most of all relief. Several ceremonies were therefore held in his memory. Here and there. So, the other night, Olga's friends mentioned him and I asked how he had killed himself. He bled himself dry in his bathtub, the day of Balzac's death. People find my interest in the details of his death unhealthy. But how do you bury someone you despised? What posture am I to adopt before that death? I won't speak any good of Hervé, I will only speak ill of him, I will speak the whole truth, my whole truth. I won't have good feelings toward him, I won't pity him. But I still find that life is heartless, life's a bitch. And he best embodied the bitchery of living.

An important thinker comes to our village to give two conferences. People rush to see him. It's only possible to see the show with tickets. There are those who have them, those who don't and, most of all, those who have never read this philosopher, he or any other. The intelligentsia of Montréal go to see Bourdieu or another the way people go to listen to Pavarotti, without conviction but with ostentation. If the organizers actually sold the tickets, I would find it less offensive, because for now, the distribution of tickets is arbitrary at best and privileges those who are members of the high society of the prevailing mediocrity and to those who have managed to maintain more or less good relations with the organizers, whom one imagines are friends of the great man and the organizers won't deny it, of that you can be certain. Montréal is the capital of swank and has no reason to envy Thomas Bernhard's Vienna when it comes to the ambition and superficiality of its elite; when visiting my 'intellectual' 'friends' (I put both words in quotation marks, but in some ways these people are more my friends than they are intellectuals, which says a lot) I always have the sense that I am attending a funeral or a wedding, which attests to my comfort levels. I recognize myself in that absolutely brilliant book of Thomas Bernhard's, *Cutting Timber*, where the narrator fights against the mediocrity afflicting the Viennese coterie. Québec has its share of timber to cut and it is well known that our country is recognized for its forests. 'Won't you be going to Bourdieu?' is the question that currently preoccupies the most insipid academics. 'My tickets came in the mail.' No, my dear, I won't go because, when it comes to snobbery, there's lots I could teach you and I would rather be killed than be caught going to Bourdieu, as you say, as you would say going to the john or to the whorehouse, in the company of people like you who never read and who barely know what they're talking about, in the company of sluts of your kind who, for months on end afterwards, will harp on that 'Bourdieu was very good, were you there?' or 'He's an enormously charismatic man, you know, he reminds me of my father, you would have liked him.' I prefer not to go to Bourdieu, Foucault (who's dead, but some don't realize it) or even Kristeva. It's stupid, but I'd rather read them. I have nothing against conferences, on the contrary, but the university in my neighbourhood stinks. People tell me it's the same everywhere. Of course, elsewhere, I don't know the people in the room. They make me laugh. People here piss me off.

There was once in my home an awful little man who dared to say, in my house, under my roof, that if Hervé, a university professor and true friend, died of AIDS, he asked for it. When I asked him to leave my table, this awful little man seemed so surprised by my violence and my distress, which he later described as sexual. He told me that he was Palestinian, that he had friends who were doctors and that as such his remarks were objective and not full of prejudice. I nonetheless kicked the awful little man out. I may be an extremist, but how could I stand for someone to make such remarks in my house when it's in that very same house that I cry for Hervé, for all of my Hervés, while that awful little man goes to Bourdieu or Derrida, speaks out against intolerance, but dares to say what he believes to be the truth? That same awful little man is convinced that he will never get AIDS and copulates gaily without a condom, because, according to the awful little man, only sodomites get it. The awful little man is therefore not a sodomite, since he's heterosexual, which, in my very humble opinion which I put forward without having been to a Bourdieu conference, are not incompatible with one another. He prefers, says he, nature's truth, which I'll cut short by evoking 'the theory of the hole made for that sole purpose.' But that won't stop the awful little man from calling himself a 'deconstructionist.'

I give a short talk in part on Foucault in which I critique the legitimacy of speaking of AIDS or even of admitting one's illness or one's homosexuality. I am asked, 'How can you work on Foucault when rumour has it that he knowingly contaminated thousands of men by going to the baths?' How can anyone contest my ethics while pronouncing the word 'rumour'?

How am I to respond to such stupidity?

In Québec, there are more literary awards than books written. A friend commented on this and how right he was! We're all about the institution. At any cost. During a conference, a young woman innocently asked a happy recipient of one of these numerous awards, 'Your book was extensively criticized, wasn't it? Did you suffer from it?' And the winner went on about the small bitter comments she had been subjected to which must surely, yes, surely have interrupted the course of her work. It's laughable. Here, every book is greeted by an award, critics don kid gloves to speak of an author and the papers are so insipid it's best to look elsewhere for criticism, like a breath of intelligence. Robert Lévesque is the only one worth admiring with fervour.

My dead friend, Hervé, a great writer, talked about the indulgences of his critics. It nauseated him. During his short life, he won so many awards that he suspected a general conspiracy. I often told him to refuse them, to send them all packing with their pathetic approval and applause. He wasn't able to. 'I would like to be Sartre and refuse the Nobel prize, but I can't even bring myself to refuse the Thing-amajig Award, it's always that much money gained.' It's true that Hervé had AIDS, that illegal medicine is costly, and that Québécois critics enabled him to extend his life by several months as well as that of his lover, Jean-Marie. Here, awards exist to make up for the fact that it is almost impossible on

Québécois soil to live by one's pen. Sartre's gesture could only come from a bourgeois in relatively good health or else is a privilege for those who live in civilized societies where medicine is free and especially less regulated.

I have to go to a Parisian café to meet a renowned writer and editor of a series, who read a piece I sent her. Here she is before me, gauging me, looking, she tells me, to see if my piece is a fluke or if I have what it takes to be a writer, a real one. Besides the fact that I find her novels completely dull, her competence in matters of the human soul seems more than questionable. How will she be able to tell in twenty minutes if I'll be able to hold the road, if I'll become as famous and useless a writer as she? She seems to doubt my capacity for insipidness and searches despairingly for tangible proof of my future, which projects me into nothingness. She speaks to me of the last award she received. Am I award material? How old am I? The great writer ends up confiding to me 'because she likes me' that I will have a very hard time making it because of the gay boy's club. 'Everything revolves around them … ' The critics are all implicated as well and will only defend young men they want to fuck. The famous author has the kindness to warn me and tell me that the road will be paved with talentless gay men who will always be more famous than me. She is thinking, of course, of my friend Hervé, who is dead, more famous than she and whom she must detest more than anything. What can I say to this talentless woman? What can I explain to her and where to begin? I say nothing, of course. I haven't the courage to tell her how much contempt I have for her. I won't write her name down here, but I know that she will read me, that she will recognize herself in my words, because she is scrambling to avoid the moment when she will lose her stardom. She spends her life reading the works of new writers in order to anticipate the end of her reign. I want provoke her by saying,'There, it's done!' She is obsessed with identifying the moment of her fall. The secret of her name, she and I will share, indefinitely. We will have at least that much in common.

The poisoned narrative is a genre in need of reinventing.

And yet, I have little to say. Very little to say and even cruelty doesn't give me much satisfaction. I never know whether to continue to write and I tell myself that if I really had something to say, I would do like Mallarmé, I would encrypt it. Because the thing to say would be unbearable, impossible. I write to distract my pain, so as not to speak of it. I cheat myself and I know it. But my pain is so silent or so set against me, that I often have the impression that it is swallowing me, swallowing me whole. My pain is a whale and I am curled into it like a Jonah. In this week's *Paris-Match*, I read these two lines from Angelo Rinaldi and Yann Queffélec: 'The novel is a nervous breakdown dominated by grammar' and 'Does an artist who doesn't commit suicide deserve to be taken seriously?' I know that I write so as not to have another breakdown but that I may have to kill myself at the end of the line, despite everything. I write to distract all the suicides and all the dead who endlessly call.

The death-line doesn't stop ringing, messages keep coming in at mavrik@sprint.ca.

Do I answer?

I went to the acupuncturist because of a pain on my right side, not the side where the heart is. My body is always in pain, and I think of Hervé Guibert whom I absorbed into me like a sponge, I spent too long marinating in his books. He thought he had found the cause of his various discomforts: spasmophilia. All his life he was a hypochondriac, which didn't stop him from dying of AIDS. People always laugh at hypochondriacs, otherwise known as imaginary invalids. But psychosomatic illness, as some people call it, was for Guibert a prescience of his death, a sort of rehearsal for the great closing act. Guibert's discomforts were foreshadowings of his end. Rather than think of the unconscious as a mechanism turned exclusively toward repeating the past, it must be understood as a process anticipating knowledge of the future. Rehearsing, as in a theatre, the scene of one's agony through the course of one's life, allows the subject to absorb the shock, to prepare for the thing. You'll tell me that by rehearsing the scene, one creates it. I don't believe in the superstition of the illness we fabricate for ourselves.

I think we often have an unconscious intuition of our death and that's what allows us to move forward in life.

On my way to the acupuncturist, I nonetheless relived a piece of my past. I had the disturbing impression of being at my psychoanalyst's, ten years earlier. It's the ceremony, the ritual, that gives that impression: the absence of a bell at the door, waiting one's turn, the recumbent position, I don't know. I began to cry, with all of those needles planted there in my body, awakening the pain of the past. For ten years, I haven't had the slightest nostalgia for psychoanalysis, I never wanted to return or even think about it; when I decided to go and lie on the couch, I was in a state of emergency, of panic and unbearable horror, and for me, leaving analysis was breaking with that period of my life. Leaving meant living at last and forgetting even the place that had helped to return me to life.

I think that I have been utterly ungrateful and unfaithful and I can write that with great pride, because for me, that unfaithfulness is a sign of health, of the precarious health of my depressive being. So when I stretched out on the acupuncturist's table and had to speak a tiny bit about myself and voices became low and muffled, I thought of those years on the couch, those years spent shouldering my death and all the deaths of my family, of my brotherhood, of my race, and I thought of Ulysses returning to Ithaca, the land of his birth, and there was no escaping returning.

I won't return to analysis, but I will never be done taking care of myself and cradling all of these deaths in me. And analysis has become one more death to care for.

Every night I walked on thousands of graves, open-sky graves that drew me to them with each step. These were often dead whom I didn't know but who demanded explanations or told me riddles I couldn't solve. In psychoanalysis, it had been necessary, one by one, to bury all of those people, and there was a mad rush out of the graves. Some were strong, some were wicked: I smothered them.

Gently, but firmly. I had to make my mind into a cemetery through which I could walk peacefully and even create a bit of order there if need be. My dead are not easy and they tend to make noise at night, but I have tamed them – now they listen to me and show me respect.

They mustn't be allowed to win, not yet.

Last night I dreamt of Hervé. I was being shown his photograph. A photograph taken in the world of the dead. Hervé held a child in his arms. I was very happy that he had had a child over there. I saw that Hervé could at last grow old and become a father. After the death of my cousin, his sister told me that most difficult of all would be growing old while her dead brother remained eternally young. The dead do not age with us. Now Tina is much older than her brother was at the time of his death. She has become the big sister. It's up to her to assume the responsibilities of head of the family and to take care of everything: putting flowers on the grave and maintaining contact between herself and her brother. One day, she will become his mother, and then his grandmother. But when she dies, she hopes Hervé will resume his position as big brother and that he'll come and comfort her at her time of dying. That's what she hopes for, at the time of her death.

Who collects the little children who die? Often someone from a very far-off generation, someone the child doesn't know. Which accounts for that sense of vengeance, of original, ancestral violence. A pediatrician says to those who are going to die that they will return immediately to their mother's womb. I don't believe this theory. Death is not regression, return. It is pathway, it is wandering, but there are people there to guide us toward nowhere. When I die,

I want my dog, Sud, with my cat, Méditerranée, on her back, to come and collect me. It's the only way I can envision truly dying. With my animals. In fact, I can confirm that my passion for animals is contemporaneous with my resignation to the scandal of death. I have found a way to rationalize and now I accept the idea that we die. Before, before the deaths of my friends, I simply didn't believe in it. Or not altogether. Or maybe yet, I revolted so much against this idea which tore me up incessantly. I rebelled against death. I thought I could annihilate it. In time, I came to understand that I had perhaps won several battles against death, but that I would lose the war.

People often reproach Olga and me for being too rich, rich especially of a fortune whose origins are questionable.

I have nothing to hide. This money, Olga and I owe entirely to several Hervés who made us their heirs, and I am proud of it. Some people think that I have something of Jean-Marie Le Pen and that I like to pilfer from the dying. I am seen as a grim reaper of people with AIDS and some will reproach me this book, saying that I am once again drawing a narcissistic revenue from the deaths of others. What can I do? Heirs of all of our Hervés, the richest and the poorest, Olga and I pay the price. How many Hervés have we watched die? How many have we kept alive? How many have we helped pass to the side of the dead? I am inclined, ironically, to say that in our entourage, it isn't always good to be called Hervé. One of our Hervés, perhaps the most affluent of the lot, used to call us his little girls, then, when his illness struck him down, he called us his little orphans. It's isn't always pleasant to go to all the funeral services. Olga and I can't take much more of our too-black clothes, our too-often-red eyes and our perpetually downturned mouths. We are often seen as vulgar undertakers or modern-day gravediggers. Sometimes, we are overcome with inexplicable crying fits. Mourning is our life. The Hervés chose us.

Every day our AIDS family is increasingly decimated and money is all that is left of our Hervés — money that substitutes as a funeral urn, ash money that we squander, scatter across the world, associations, in keeping with the last wishes of an Hervé.

Shortly before his death, Hervé called us in the middle of the night. It was the eve of his birthday which we were to celebrate with him and a few other Hervés. I didn't recognize his voice on the telephone, but I knew it was serious. I hate for the phone to ring in the night, it makes me shudder, because when it rings, it's that someone is close to death. 'Catherine, my dear, I'm not doing at all well, could you come with Olga? I need you,' murmured Hervé, his voice breaking. Hervé was suffering from irremediable tuberculosis, as do many people with AIDS. He was spitting up blood, a basinful, when we arrived at his place. The household domestics weren't there and I opened the door with my key, the very key Hervé had placed in my left hand one day, declaring with the solemnity of a prophet, 'You will soon need it.' He had also immediately closed my fingers around the keys, deliberately, slowly, to indicate that I wasn't to lose them. Then, he held my hands in his for some five minutes while he playfully told me about a new variety of orchid he had finally managed to procure. That night, Hervé almost died, but he wouldn't let Olga and me call an ambulance that would take him to the hospital. 'I don't want to die in hospital,' he said to me on many occasions. That night, Hervé clung to Olga and me. He held us with all the strength left in his shrunken body. He vomited all of his blood onto us and covered us in his excrement as well. I know that Hervé never recovered from having done that to us. This man, who was so refined, so polished, allowed himself, that night, to become a child before us. He didn't concern himself with contamination, he who panicked at the slightest little germ, but with the indecency of his body. For him, the real horror was having shown us his degeneration. But he couldn't go back. Hervé was incapable of killing himself and he needed someone to assist him before death. And he chose us, Olga and me, to accompany him. I never knew why we were elected by Hervé, why he wanted it to be us. I don't think I ever intimated that I was prepared for such trials, and Olga, little Olga, even less so than I. In fact, I am certain that we were unprepared, and we remain so to this day. But one doesn't escape destiny. And I didn't escape mine.

That night, Hervé didn't die. He died another night, the night Olga and I 'helped him die.' Is it possible to help someone die? Is it possible to facilitate death? I don't know, but that's what we say, that's how we come to accept it. Must I say that I am fiercely opposed to euthanasia and that I will remain so until my death? Until my own death, but not that of my friends. I hate that doctors or the State have the power to decide whether we should die. But since I am in favour of suicide and since Hervé admitted to me that he dreamt of it, without having the courage, and since he simply asked for our help, I could only say yes.

'I will only kill myself when it will no longer be possible, my dears, I will only kill myself just before the end, but I will need "help,"' Hervé said to us one day in March in his greenhouse among all his flowering orchids. We 'helped' Hervé die. We 'helped him abbreviate his suffering,' so as 'not to die in hospital.' How can I put it? Of course, every word becomes suspect, quickly, very quickly, in my own eyes, and no one is more suspicious of me than I am. But I would be even more suspect to myself if I hadn't helped Hervé with his death, if I had said no, if I hadn't been there. We are the heirs of this man whom we 'helped' or maybe simply assassinated. What do I know? But I am responsible for my Hervés to the very end. And if I must plead guilty, I will.

All my life, crackpots have been drawn to me. I have a crazy charisma or something along those lines, and if a lunatic shows up at a dinner party or a get-together, he's mine. I should have been a psychiatrist; mental institutions would be overflowing with psychotics, the city on the whole would be more normal. For now, hordes of lunatics congregate at my door, they harrass me, arrive unannounced, cram me full of the craziest of gifts, of course, which range from perfumed sanitary napkins to ice cream spoons. I am adulated.

Certainly, I am fascinated by madness, by Artaud, by Gauvreau, but all of my lunatics are starting to smother me and, more and more, I find myself throwing fits of rage against all of these people who get on my nerves, who assail me, who need a good spectator, someone who knows how to laugh at the comedy of their madness.

Lunatics like to be laughed at. Lunatics have a sense of humour and want to be seen as mad. What people always forget when they think about lunatics is that they are also perverse, and manipulative games are not uncommon to them. A lunatic is no more real than a neurotic; he lies just as much as other people and needs to act out his symptoms. He plays for us and he plays with us. That's why it's important to be wary of the lunatic and not allow him to encroach on the small territories of our reason out of which we're being endlessly cheated. The lunatic dreams of having us enter into his system; he needs someone to believe in his delirium, someone to say yes, someone who shares in his lunacy, so that the lunatic is not alone struggling in his world of lunatics, so that the lunatic ceases to be a lunatic. The lunatic is entrancing. If he manages to convince us that he is not as much of a lunatic as all that, he will have won. And the lunatic has time, all the time in the world, something neurotics don't have. The lunatic wears us down through erosion and hypnosis. It is therefore important to guard against lunatics.

My first contact with a lunatic goes back to high school, when Jana admitted to me that she wasn't a communist. At fifteen, we were all communists and this dissidence was enough to get me thinking. But Jana's staunch capitalism wasn't her only symptom; she was fixated on Pope Paul VI, whom she wanted to assassinate. In her eyes, the person responsible for Vatican II was the bastard par excellence. He had changed the Church and Jana couldn't forgive him for it. She always carried a knife around with her that she would drop on the ground, inadvertently, when she dug into her schoolbag to pull out her math book or her French book. Furthermore, Jana was a revisionist and laid into the history teacher when she evoked World War II and the Holocaust, which, at the time, was still referred to as the extermination of the Jews. Jana turned red with rage, called the teacher a liar and stormed out, slamming the door behind her while screaming insults in Polish. Jana was Polish, but no one had ever met her parents and maybe she didn't have any. She didn't last long in our high school; the threats she uttered to students and teachers earned her a quick dismissal and this, despite the intervention of the Latin teacher with whom she kidded in the language of the Vatican. She called me from time to time, waited for me on my way home and told me that I was the only one who understood her, that I was the only true communist, that I didn't do it for show and that I was therefore the first to be converted, before anyone else. It didn't take much more for me to feel flattered and, even though Jana horrified me, I continued to talk to her from time to time, even when her eyes were bloodshot and she was foaming at the mouth. Often, I tried in vain to rid myself of her, but she liked me a lot and one day she placed her lips over mine to seal the pact of our friendship. Jana took my hands in hers and twisted my wrists to fully pour her fervent words into me. She read the life of Saint Thérèse of Lisieux and recited long passages while comparing me to Sister What's-her-name, worthy friend of the saint.

I was afraid of Jana, while at the same time subjugated by her power. She ate bread and continually drank wine (she must have found God there more than anywhere else), and I was fascinated by her resistance to alcohol and the absence of fear in her life. My mother adored her and thought that I had at last found a proper friend, a believer, a nice young girl. Jana wasn't interested in boys, of course; she found it immoral to keep their company. She wanted to be pope and everyone thought she was a lesbian, but for me she was simply a lunatic, and lesbianism was too simple a description for the state of mental confusion in which Jana found herself. One day, she saw me leaving a meeting of left-wing students to which, in her words, she had prohibited me from going. But I had misunderstood her good will and gone to the meeting unthinkingly. She caught me as I was walking through the door of the premises and swore at me in Polish, which has made that language irremediably unpleasant to me. She told me she should kill me, that I didn't deserve to live, but that she would spare me because God was asking the trial of forgiveness. I became even more afraid of her, but she left and I didn't see her again.

She called my mother from time to time to ask about me and my mother sent her photographs of me. My mother never forgave me for having lost such a good friend, and I suspect that she and Jana met several times. My mother isn't a believer, but she likes pissing me off and interfering with my life. It's the teenager in me that's still speaking, that rebellious teenager who forgives nothing.

Jana called me when John Paul II became pope. The fact that a Pole was at the Vatican renewed her hope in life and she decided to join a sect of visionaries that I won't name, because I don't want to pull the same stunt Rushdie did and find myself with a Catholic fatwa on my back. 'With John Paul II, I know it's a sign, I'll be pope soon,' Jana assured me before hanging up on me, even though she was the one who called. Ten years later, I saw her in a newspaper, where she was photographed chained to a post, near an American abortion clinic. I recognized her right away, even though she was carrying in her hands a bowl containing a fetus in formaldehyde, which I found rather perverse. The article explained that she was wanted, because she was suspected of having murdered an abortion doctor in his home, stabbed nineteen times. I followed the story, but learned that the inquest had reached the conclusion that Jana wasn't the murderer. As for me, I believe she did it because of the nature of the weapon used in the crime. My theory's as good as any other. Two years ago, Jana left a message on my answering machine telling me that she had been kicked out of her sect because she had had the courage to tell her superior the truth and that the pope would soon die so that she could take his place.

I know that she is capable of anything, since she is capable of finding my unlisted telephone number, even though I have changed my name since high school and since she's been carrying fetus bowls around with her. But I don't know who to warn, and I tell myself that the director of the sect, more interested than I am in the pope's survival, is well-informed. Let him warn his peers.

I think that Jana will always find me when she wants to, that I am not rid of her yet and that in the beyond, I'll be stuck with her again. That's what's called a destiny. But together we'll plot God's assassination so that she can take his place.

I am being interviewed on the radio about a vaguely theoretical book I wrote. I have to go through my big book again
the night before the radio show. What might I have written? I don't remember anything well. I am amnesic when it
comes to my writing, and I think that I write to forget, to
relieve my memory. A friend who read my book is encour-
aging. 'Your book is funny, you'll enjoy yourself,' she says.
The word 'funny' has a strange ring to my ear. It seemed to
me that my book was about death, I wonder how I might
have been funny. I must have missed the overall effect.
Little matter, I must go through my book again and those
of the two other guests. Strangely, I have the impression of
having greater affinity with the theories in the other
guests' books than that which I must assume as my own
theory. And why did I have to go and make such an enormous book? I must have written under hypnosis. Who
spoke through me?

I am responsible for this mastodon of a book. It's really
the same as with a child, we are responsible even if he doesn't
at all look like us. I tell myself next time I'll keep it short.

I saw an interview with Deleuze. Eight hours spent
watching him in a movie theatre. He spoke to us from the
beyond, since he granted the interview on the sole condition
that it be aired posthumously. To speak in life as the dead one
will become. There was a look of amusement and perversion

in Deleuze's eyes. The dead are always somewhat perverse. They laugh at we poor living, always attempting to encircle death. Deleuze played dead and, well, he was quite convincing. At times, he came back to life, but not for too long. Intermittently. He told us that we must write for animals, children or lunatics — in other words, in the place of animals, children or lunatics. Me, I write for the dead. In the place of the dead. It's not that I'm an excellent medium, or that I have greater talent than others to chat with the dead. It's that, like Deleuze, I am a bit perverse, I play dead and I don't think I do too badly in that role.

In the last two films I saw, Abel Ferrara's *The Funeral* and Téchiné's *Les Voleurs*, some of the actors must in fact play dead. They are lying in coffins and have taken on the posture of 'death.' It's not the easiest role to play. It requires a certain amount of talent, I think, and a fair bit of perversion especially.

I have a new friend. That, at any rate, is what I believe. Regardless, I have the impression that he and I are beginning something very important these days, something that will last or end tragically. There are people with whom only intense things happen, with whom the world becomes more powerful. I have that sense with Hervé. It's physical, it's like a car accident in which the steering wheel hits me right in the thorax. Every time I see him, that very violence is at hand. I don't know if he experiences the same thing, if our encounters plunge him into the same state. In fact, I don't think that's what he wants, I don't think he's up to it. I carry that violence for the two of us. And then there are moments of extreme softness, moments when nothing happened, during which, together, we tame, very gently, almost tenderly, the idea of a catastrophe. Perhaps simply that of a friendship that will not take place or that will disintegrate by its own violence.

I am thinking of Lady Diana and her encounter with Dodi Al Fayed. They shared the brutality of their death from the moment they met. And the accidental driver, Henri Paul, is a sort of Iphigenia sacrificed for the arrival of death, for the violent march of destiny to follow its course. Some see him as entirely responsible. The responsibility for death is a preoccupation of the living. On the other side, in the world of the dead, the orders of destiny are accomplished; one makes the gestures to which one is constrained. Even Diana's bodyguard said that Henri Paul had a likeable air about him. This man is not a monster but a tragic character, the very figure of destiny. And his body, prevented by autopsies and inquests from finding rest, remains in excess. Destiny must be embodied and this embodiment remains an indecent, almost obscene matter. My friend Angela, who loved her mother more than all else in the world, even ended up forgiving her father for having murdered her. There is, of course, something inhumane about writing that down, but death is not made for humans – it is ignoble, inhumane, and it's necessary to come to terms with playing along.

I don't understand Dodi's father who, on the day of his son's death, thinks of prosecuting the paparazzi. I don't understand the issue of responsibility for death, especially at such a time. It's as though the father hadn't wanted to cross the boundary separating the living from the dead, if only for time enough to briefly mourn.

We musn't approach death with our criteria of the living, with the notion of justice, of rights, of reparation. The death of someone close should drag us into the logic of the dead, even if it means losing our head, even if it costs us our life. It is necessary, for a time, to pass through to the other side of the mirror. Period. Legal battles, inquests, declarations of war, should be prohibited for at least a year to those who are suffering. Their only allowable recourse might be murder. They could even be provided with assistance to weep, they could be placed in ignoble quarantine, and the living prohibited from approaching them, from speaking to them. People in mourning are on the side of death and I approve of the aversion the living sometimes feel toward them.

This very book is contaminated by death and if it is treated like a pariah, I will understand.

Nonetheless, I choose my friends according to their words of consolation, those they will speak when everything goes wrong. I love them for that. Angela will be there, of course. Emmanuelle as well, she will find words, and Daniel, who doesn't yet know how to find them, will sit beside me blinking nervously. I will be able to cry violently into his gentle eyes.

I envy Diana for having been buried pregnant. I have always been scared to death of finding myself alone in my coffin. But Diana is with her child for all eternity and this image consoles me completely. Diana's brother, Earl Spencer, remains, for me, an admirable person, even though he may well be the worst possible bastard. He is a modern-day Antigone.

Henceforth, we no longer mourn our brothers, and even if we continue to condemn the violence and indifference of monarchs in the face of death, we suffer instead for his sister. Yes, Lord Spencer is an Antigone, and history is merely changing sexes. Some call this progress.

Sometimes, when I am unable to write or to cry, I do a tarot reading. In the world of cards, I make peace with death. There are images to represent it. Tarot reassures me and even when I come up against the worst, I stay aloof, I become a medium. Medium: that's the profession I would most likely have held during the nineteenth century. I would have been a oracle among the Greeks or even a cursed Cassandra. Today, I could be an astrologer, Nancy Reagan's, Yeltsin's or the Pope's. I could even come up with something that would predict the future on the Internet. But I decided to write, it's my way of making contact with the beyond. I breathe the emanations of writing deeply into myself, I drug myself on the dust of my computer screen. I have become she through whom death arrives.

Some two weeks before her death, Diana and Dodi consulted with her appointed seer, who must have predicted divorce, splendour and love. I seem to recall it having been August 13th. What happened on that day? What was said? Did the seer see? Did she speak? Or did she simply and purely screw up? If that's the case, I think that she should have considered suicide ... just like the magnetic healer Hervé Guibert consulted before his death, the one who said that AIDS wouldn't win. He, too, must certainly have thought of abridging his days. It's not that I believe these people to be charlatans. On the contrary. But when you make that big a mistake, you've got to have the modesty to believe there's something in it, that the other person, the client, has become your own encounter with death. You've got to find within you the humility to read your own death in the other. After such a failure, you've got to be able to decode and understand one last time the meaning of symbols. We cease, then, to be mediums or mediators of death, but we understand whose turn it is to receive the announcement of the worst. In the logic of the living, I imagine that if there is someone to prosecute in the story of Diana, it's not the paparazzi, but the seer. She didn't do her job: either she didn't see or she didn't offer help to someone in danger. In the logic of the dead, that which seers use, the medium must understand that her time is up and that Diana was her own death card.

I have always refused to go to seers, because I fear their fear of me. I am my own black cat, I bring bad luck to all those who see into me, because I read them far too easily. It's not a matter of arrogance or immodesty. I, too, will encounter the card of death, but it won't fear me. It makes me think of that magnificent film by Pedro Almodovar in which the main protagonist, a matador, has his palm read by a gypsy. Since he knows that he is going to die in the following hours and that the terrified gypsy sees it very clearly in the hand he holds out to her, the matador winks superbly at her, with such lucidity and irony that I could never match. That seers, mediums, are terrified by those who are are going to die, there is the sign of a great destiny. To hold one's own card of death and brandish it before the faces of other people like a triumph isn't given to everyone. Must I say that I am not of that calibre?

I am angry at Hervé. He scalded one of my tropical fish, under the pretext that he wanted to help it not to suffer. Does he plan to scald the oceans, set fire to the forests, batter the dying to help them not to suffer?

Many of Hervé's friends died of AIDS. And for Hervé, what matters most is a quick death. 'He didn't suffer, you understand.' And even I who, with the help of Olga, killed a friend who was in agony, even I don't understand Hervé. He exasperates me. We do the same things, he and I, and yet I hold his actions against him. My fish didn't ask him for death. What difference would it have made if that little fish had taken four days to die and graze the bottom of the bowl? I think of myself killing a dying friend, I took part in that suffering, his and mine. And Olga's as well. Hervé scalds his own suffering and the suffering of others. With great splashes of hot water and lukewarm words. Nonetheless, I'm the one who took a big risk by killing my friend. Hervé eliminated a fish along with his contemplation of evil. He was most likely right, and I'm the one who deserves imprisonment, even if I proudly admit that I would do it again. If a friend asked me to.

Apparently, friendship is measured by the transportation of cadavers. A true friend is someone to whom one can say, 'I have a cadaver on my hands, can you help me transport it?' This true friend doesn't ask questions, doesn't ask where the cadaver comes from, nor why, nor how. My friend with AIDS asked me to transport a cadaver and that cadaver was his own. I didn't hesitate. A mover of cadavers of all kinds, that's what I have become.

Going bankrupt. This subject begins one of Violette Leduc's stories. My father went bankrupt an incalculable number of times and me, despite all the money harvested from the murders of friends, I always find myself on the verge of bankruptcy. Bad investments, terrible advice, the desire to give, and here I am once again on the verge of bankruptcy, but only on the verge. From here, I contemplate the void into which I would like to throw myself headlong. But another murder comes along, some inheritance, destiny gives a start and I don't dive. I dream of wagering the rest of my fortune at a casino. I would bet on a single number. But I'm afraid, too afraid of winning. My passion for gambling manifests itself in bankruptcy, in the game of double or nothing that I play with myself. Sometimes, as well, I fantasize that I have made a subconsciously deliberate mistake, that I did something really very shameful which will lead me to suicide. I am always playing with limits. Because that's not where death is, not in that permanent resurrection. Not in that play. Death is somewhere else and that's why I distract myself by thinking about suicide or bankruptcy. It allows me to forget.

Ivan is very much a gambler as well. He goes to the casino and tells me that he experiences a sort of sexual arousal, very intense. I understand. My father felt the same thing when the bailiffs came to seize all of our furniture or when the police came to take him to jail. At that moment, my father thought he was going to lose everything. Or else win everything. Those are the only times I ever saw him happy. There were also the hours my mother spent laying into him because she had discovered another mistress. He was jubilant not knowing whether or not he would lose my mother. With time, that pleasure faded. My father realized my mother would never leave. From that moment on, my father was never happy again.

As a gift, my father brought me a crate of oysters that he had left marinating all day in the heat in the trunk of his car. He plays double or nothing with the death of his children, but I don't know how to hold a grudge against him. That's the way he is, and his rotten oysters, he himself would eat them gluttonously. I love oysters. My mother never ate any, but she continually repeats that our passion for seafood will end up poisoning us. To be poisoned by food is to consume one's own death. Apparently, on the night of her death, Lady Diana ate sole and white asparagus. Last supper, big meal at the Ritz. I find sole very bland, but that meal all of white must surely have had something solemn about it, virginal. I don't remember what Dodi ate, I think it was salmon. They both ate fish that night and, even if people find it base that the menu of their last meal was published, it does me good to know. To think that before dying they were very much alive, to wonder whether they had deciphered any clues about their imminent death. Me, I find there's something sacred about contemplating their last night. 'Let's leave them in peace, now,' is what people are saying pretty much every-where. I don't even understand what that means.

By way of provocation, I would say that I would love to live pursued by the paparazzi. Not everyone is that fortunate. Dozens of friends have died alone in what is called dignity. It isn't necessarily more pleasant than dying in the photographer's flash. We are led to believe that it's awful to live like Diana. Is that to convince us that we are happier working every day, eating mad cow, croaking in our corner, without an entourage and with three bouquets of wilted flowers at our funeral? That's pure propaganda, brainwashing. What's more, the absence of paparazzi in our lives is no guarantee against dying in a car accident at the age of thirty-six. If monarchs and stars said that they liked the paparazzi, there would be revolutions, uprisings. To ensure social peace, better off to declare that it's tragic to be photographed while on a yacht in the middle of the Mediterranean. How stupid do we look? Unless the great people of this world are stupid enough to believe in something like private life.

I often think of all those flowers the English bought after Diana's death. I think of the destiny of those flowers, how they were recycled. Several days after the funeral, the flowers that were still healthy were distributed to sick people in hospitals, and those that had rotted were composted for the garden of the palace in which the princess had lived. It was necessary to find a way to send those flowers to Diana, dead, and people used their imaginations. Sick people have something of Diana, since she was interested in their fate, and the garden of Kensington is Diana once again. In fact, it isn't so easy to send something to the dead, and, here, I think that England did a good job. In my country, flowers are left at the church because cemeteries don't accept cut flowers. They rot, make a mess. That was the explanation given to me.

Eliminating rotting things from a cemetery seems to me like somewhat of a difficult task. But that's the sort of repression on which our society is founded. At the last funeral I attended, the body was not interred. The coffin was placed on the embankment and the gravediggers came several hours later, when their schedule allowed for it. Nonetheless, leaving the cemetery was awful. We hadn't done our job as the living, we hadn't even thrown a handful of dirt onto the coffin. That gesture is difficult to make, but it's necessary.

In fact, here, people don't cry at funerals. One musn't appear too sad … it would ruin the day.

On the contrary, we tell funny stories about the dead. To keep good memories. The joking that goes on at funerals frankly makes me want to puke. At his own funeral, Pierre Larocque had arranged for Mozart's *Requiem* to be played.

I am grateful to him for having given us permission to cry.

Pavarotti, reeling, at Diana's funeral, was grandiose. There's no doubt about it, Italians have a sense of death. Many will say that it's a comedy, a way of stealing the show. Maybe. But I prefer that to all the jokes that are told at our northern funerals. No one's going to make me believe that cheerfulness the day of one's sister's funeral is more real. That's just de la merde.

While walking Sud, I caught sight, from a distance, of a dead cat, lying on its little side. I moved closer, being sure to hold Sud's leash tightly, and I could see that this cat was wearing a collar and a tag around its fragile, too fragile neck. This cat had been hit by a car. I watched it for a long time, tears welling in my eyes. But I didn't take it into my arms, I didn't bring it home with me, I didn't touch it, nor warm it, nor pet it, nor cradle it, nor bury it. I left and I ran to the first telephone, to alert the proper authorities to come and collect the little cat. I left it there on the ground, washing my hands of the body I had found. Everyone tells me I did well, but I can't sleep anymore. The little cat haunts me. Apparently, I did the right thing, did as I should. And yet I feel ashamed. Ashamed for having done my duty and nothing more, for not having taken care of my dead. I managed death, me, the manager of funerary business. I didn't pay with my person for this encounter with death. At four in the morning, I wake up in a sweat: 'To how many friends have I done the same thing? Will someone pick me up at the edge of the road one day?' Someone's got to lay out the cadaver, and institutions, proper authorities, funeral parlours, aren't there for that. On the contrary.

Olga often talks to our friend Emmanuelle about her dead body. Olga says that she wants Emmanuelle to see her dead and Emmanuelle says that she wants Olga to see her dead. Pledges of friendship. To keep the body, watch over it, hold it, cherish it a little while longer, is that not the least we can do for our friends?

I think of all those who went to kiss the feet of Mother Teresa, all those who wanted to pay homage to her. People around me didn't stop laughing and saying that it must have started to smell terribly bad, that body, in the dead of heat, in Calcutta.

Of course it was rotting and the smell must have been practically unbearable. But perhaps loving people also means being able to breathe in the smell of their cadavers, 'the aroma of our rotted loves.'

I fell by chance, as is said on such occasions, on the self-portrait of a young woman from the sixteenth century whom I strangely resemble. Her name is Catherine Van Hemessen and her self-portrait is dated 1540, if I have correctly read the words she drew in the left corner of the painting. 'EGO, CATERINA DE HEMESSEN ME PINXI 1540. ETATIS SUA 20.' So she was twenty years old at the time of this little painting, if she's not lying about her age, because I am as suspicious of her as I am of myself. I know very little about her and it's all mixed up in my head: Caterina was from Leyden; the painting is now in Basel; her father, Jean, was a painter; her sister's name was Cristina and her husband's, Christian. I saw another of Catherine's paintings at London's National Gallery. I may have read somewhere that she specialized in women's portraits. What else is there to say about this resemblance? As much as I scrutinize the crumbs of Caterina's life, I see nothing. And yet when I look at her, it's as though I were seeing myself in a mirror. It's me in sixteenth-century dress. Even her crossed eyes are mine done in an old-fashioned way. I wonder sometimes if, as she painted herself, Catherine created an image that resembled her. Maybe in reality, I only look like this portrait and not at all like Caterina, who was, herself, much more beautiful. Did she see me on that day? Was she a seer of me, the way one sees a utopia, a dystopia? I would have preferred to find a twin in a painting that wasn't a self-portrait. I could have convinced myself that I had previously been a beauty ideal and that some painter had ardently desired to paint a woman like me. I console myself with the thought that in a self-portrait, one always has to make do with nature, which isn't always generous. And then, finding myself in a self-portrait I obviously didn't paint is a little discomfiting to the mind.

I often examine Caterina. Her large doe eyes and her somewhat foolish expression don't provide any answers. Once again, I see a good likeness. On the other hand, I am a very poor painter, self-portraits or portraits period. I work with clay. It's very messy. I mould recumbent sculptures, of course. I have a great passion for sephulchral figures: recumbent or orant. They are often lots of fun and not at all life-like. At Westminster Abbey, at York Minster, I saw some that were very funny. A recumbent figure with his recumbent dog (which made me wonder whether the dog had been buried with the master or if it was simply symbolic) and little figurines of roughly thirty centimetres decorating the built-in crypts prayed for eternity. Veritable little tomb-dolls. Caterina reminds me of these figurines made of wood, clay or stone, kneeling in homage to the dead. Her self-portrait is nothing approaching funereal, but there is something ridiculously minuscule about her. Her hands, her body, everything seems narrow. Only her head is immoderately fat. It's as though she were a real person, but shrunken. That's what is so amusing to me about the figurines on English graves. They are human beings in miniature. It's as though, through their orant solemnity, the wooden pygmies were demonstrating to me the grotesqueness of death. I want to laugh when I see them, to kiss them, to take them into my arms and then destroy them with a violent blow, without warning. They are so small, I'd make short work of them. When I see Catherine, I have the same feeling. I want very badly to hurt her after having spent a few good minutes laughing at her. Every time it's the same thing. For many reasons, Catherine reminds me of how arbitrary our bodies are, hers, but mine especially, and one day or another, she'll have to pay for that.

Tonight, I'm going dancing. I'll put on shoes that Véronique and Ivan gave me before leaving for Italy. Wonderful Italian shoes that give me a bouncy step and will remind me of them all year long. Shoes that make me light and have the power to make me exist in the echo of my feet. Shoes worthy of Saint-Denys Garneau's poem 'Accompaniment.' I'll go dancing with Olga on this All Saints' Day. Tonight, it's my birthday, and I feel bewitched by my seven-league shoes. I'll dance for all my dead, but also to celebrate my existence, my own birth. 'I exist, that's all, ' declared Ludovic, who hates talk of the dead and prefers to frighten them. Tonight, we won't talk of the dead. We'll dance for them, but also to celebrate our bodies. We'll make the dead jealous. I promised Olga. That's the way it is. It must be done. It's our lot, as the living. We've got to respect it.

So, let the dead be jealous.

Hervé died yesterday.

And so, last night, I went to paradise. There was a strand of fine sand, very white, and before me, the white expanse of a freezing, foaming sea. A chalky haze covered the beach and the waves. I was in the middle of nowhere, at the world's end, on the edge of the continents, and I walked wearing a pair of pants and a navy blue sweater. Like in a blue and white film. I lost myself in the colour of the sand, the ocean, but at the same time, I resisted it. I awaited my mother. She got lost at sea January 7, 1997, off the coast of Chile. A white whale whose shape I glimpsed in the distance would soon spit her back up. At the edge of the sea, I await my mother. 'Return my mother's body to me,' I repeated throughout the dream, but the dream didn't go anywhere. There was no more time, or only time. By dint of walking, my bare feet traced some useless hieroglyphic on the wet sand, I came across the hull of a little red wooden boat on the white background of which these blue words were painted: 'Deus no sabe o teu destino.'

A big white tarp cloaked the bottom of the ship. I lifted it gradually, slowly. In the hold, I recognized Hervé, his perfectly white body curled up, almost a child. I tried in vain to awaken him and had to realize that Hervé was dead. That, even in paradise, convinced as I was of being there, my friends were dead, my mother, absent. 'God doesn't know your destiny. 'I took my place at Hervé's side; I wrapped my arms around him and suddenly started to become very pale, erasing myself in the hostile white of the world. I was going to disappear, finally, to be swallowed up. I became indistinguishable from the revolting white matter of the air. There were no more words, no more bodies, nothing. All the dead died in me. In turn, the white faded away. I was dead. At last.

This dream troubled me. Deeply. What surprises me in all of this is my passivity. I cannot live without the idea of seeing all of my dead one day, without thinking of an afterwards, of a becoming in death, and yet … Yet, in my dream, I accepted with delectation the idea of an evanescent void, a vast ghost of death. It makes my skin crawl. People who speak of returning from the dead often speak of a serene acceptance of the beyond. I have always found this resignation scandalous. And here I am, just as servile as the rest. Ready to melt into the great viscous white. Everything tends to erase itself. The traces blur quickly. I know it, and for that, I am disgusted at myself.

One day, we will all be dead, me and all of my own. Others will speak for us, in our place, will commemorate us or forget us all at once. There's no certainty. There is a knowing and that's something. I could review all of my dead, draw up lists of those I have loved, carry in me all the dead of the world, have their surnames tattooed onto the entire surface of my glorious body, erect millions of monuments, have a thousand children named after those who disappeared without me, spend every second of my days and nights reciting the names of the forgotten; one day or another, everything, and I mean everything, will erase itself, will. And despite myself, this thought fills me with complete happiness. I am sometimes so tired of commemorating.

Let it stop one day, let it end, let there be no more talk of my rendezvous with the dead.

Acknowledgements

The translator acknowledges the assistance of the Banff International Literary Translation Centre 2003 residency program at the Banff Centre in Alberta, Canada and the support offered by a British Centre for Literary Translation residential bursary and the EC Culture 2000 program.

The publisher and translator would like to thank the Canada Council for the Arts Translation Grants program for making this translation possible.

About the Author

Catherine Mavrikakis is a professor of literature at the Université de Montréal. This book, published in French in 2000 by Editions TROIS as *Deuils cannibales et mélancoliques*, is her first novel. She has also published the novel *Ça va aller* and, with Martine Delvaux, the epistolary fiction *Ventriloquies*. She is working on a third novel, called *Flore-du-crachet*.

About the Translator

Nathalie Stephens writes in English and French and sometimes neither. She is the author, notably, of *Paper City* (Coach House), *Je Nathanaël* (l'Hexagone), *Somewhere Running* (Arsenal Pulp), *Colette m'entends-tu?* (TROIS) and *This Imagined Permanence* (Gutter). *UNDERGROUND* (TROIS) was shortlisted in 2000 for the Grand Prix du Salon du livre de Toronto. In 2002, Nathalie was awarded a Chalmers Arts Fellowship. Excerpts from her work have been translated into Slovene. On occasion, she translates herself.

Typeset in Spectrum, and printed and bound at the Coach House on bpNichol Lane, 2004

Edited and designed by Alana Wilcox
Cover by Rick/Simon
Cover image, *Venir (Cimetière Montparnasse, 2003)*, by Martine
    Audet, courtesy of the artist

Coach House Books
401 Huron St. (rear) on bpNichol Lane
Toronto, Ontario
M5S 2G5

416 979 2217
1 800 367 6360

mail@chbooks.com
www.chbooks.com